Time
Waver

To Alexis,
I know you don't read often, but I hope you
read this! I don't know much about you which
is unfortunate but what I do know is pretty
great. You're going to make a wonderful nurse
in the future and I was wondering if you
can steal me a tortoise from your workplace
now. Jk! Lets go hunt for alaskan klee kai
and set matching puppies! Hopefully I'll see you
around sometime!

Daniel Doan

Copyright © 2014 Daniel Doan
All rights reserved.
ISBN-13: 9780990562405
ISBN-10: 0990562409
Library of Congress Control Number: 2014912888
Daniel Doan, Garden Grove, CA

Acknowledgements

FOR MY FAMILY, who stuck by me through all my trying times. Without their support, I would not have the tools or motivation to pursue my education and my writing. My parents, who gave everything and more for their children. My brothers, who indulged my creative spirit by reshaping our reality into fantasy.

For N.D., who was there step-by-step of the way and encouraged me to follow my dreams. Her love and comfort are my two pillars that keep me standing. I would not know where I would be without her.

For the Peter's Posse, who without a doubt made me the man I am today. Thank you for embracing my eclectic ways and providing a wonderful friendship that I'm sure will last a lifetime.

And last but not least, for all my readers who stuck with me through this whirlwind of a ride. I couldn't have finished this book without you. If you weren't there to read it, I wouldn't be here right write it.

Time
Waver

1
Meeting the Doc

MY NAME IS Blake Dawson, and as of right now, I have become the most promising student in my senior class at Cristo Rey High School—Cristo Rey for short. I didn't become the best because I was naturally gifted in the head, and definitely not because my study habits were above and beyond. I was at the top of the education pyramid because simply, I can travel back in time.

How it came about is a long story: it all began on a Friday. It wasn't just any Friday; it was test day in history class. And I was late. First, the alarm didn't go off. Second, my car wouldn't start. It was countless blocks to school, at one of the busiest times for New York streets. The sidewalks were crowded with the hustle and bustle of people striving to make a living in the city. The air was damp from the morning moisture but the twenty-first century smog eclipsed that dawning tranquility. I hurried along, grumbling with one eye looking out for human obstacles and the other on my broken watch. The outer casing was cracked—don't recall how it happened—but the digital numbers still showed up fine. I pulled in a deep breath, realizing that I had about ten minutes before my first class started and I was still about fifteen blocks away. My mood plummeted further as the idea of a marked down test slowly pitted itself in my stomach. Stomping my feet with every step, I lost sight of the road and almost bumped into someone.

He stood there looking at a tree, waving his arms like a maniac.

"Get down here." He sounded like he wanted to yell but kept his voice at a perfect volume. "Don't you just sit there and purr all day. I have plenty of things to do."

The tree held particular interest to the man. At first, I didn't see what he was looking for, and then I caught a glimpse of a wagging tail. I inched closer and a cat came into view. A small one, white in color and it seemed to enjoy teasing its owner.

I skidded to a stop and wondered why the man didn't climb the tree and grab his cat. It wasn't that big of a tree but then again, the branches looked unstable. The man looked to be over the peak in years. Gray hairs sticking out like needles in a cactus. His outfit was a three-piece suit, slightly wrinkled and oversized but well groomed, nonetheless. I glanced down at my watch again and sighed. I was late already, so there was no harm spending a few minutes helping this man. The cold air stiffened my hands so I blew hot breath into them. The rush of heat tingled my nerves and gave my fingers feeling again.

"Sir." I stepped in. "I'll get the cat for you."

He smiled and nodded.

I stretched my arms over my head and grabbed a handful of branches. Once my grip felt secure, I hoisted into the tree. The rough bark scratched against my skin and the moisture in the air didn't help with getting a strong foothold in the wood's pockets. It took a moment to reach the cat, which chose to remain still and wide-eyed, surrendering to its imminent capture without a hint of hostility. I curled one hand around the cat and brought it down carefully, dropping it into the man's arms before patting the dirt off my clothes.

"There you go, sir. Have a nice day." I turned to walk away.

"Now wait a minute, son. I think you deserve some compensation." The man stroked the cat in his arms. "What's your name, young sir?" He spoke as if he belonged in an earlier time period.

I turned back. "Blake, Blake Dawson, sir." I mimicked the man's politeness.

"Well Blake, my boy, people here call me Doc Primo. It's a pleasure to make your acquaintance."

This conversation was dragging. But I didn't have the heart to stop the old man. "Yes sir, quite the pleasure."

He laughed. "So Blake, shouldn't you be in school right now?"

"Well, yeah, I'm running a little late," I admitted sheepishly. "I should probably get going." As I turned and paced away, the cat dropped from the man's arms and trotted by me, brushing against my leg and purring with joy.

Doc Primo trailed and picked up the cat again. He must've caught sight of my broken watch because it served as the next conservation topic.

"Now Blake, how are you supposed to tell time with all those fracture lines cutting across your watch?"

I shrugged. "Well, I guess that explains why I'm late to class now, doesn't it?" I was growing agitated. I didn't care if I sounded rude or not now.

"Time is a tricky concept, isn't it? Such an abstract idea, yet everything revolves around it. It's like an intangible master, chaining all of us to its will. Wouldn't you agree, Blake?"

"I guess. Sure."

"What do you think of time travel, Blake?"

I thought for a moment. "It would be a useful tool to have," I replied simply.

He smiled as if that was the answer he was looking for. "Now, what would you say if I could bestow this power onto you?" His eyes skewered mine as if he wanted to peer into my soul. "You helped return my precious pet, the least I can do is offer you something in return."

"What are you talking about?" I asked, confused.

"What would you say if I can give you the power to go back in time?"

"That would be great." A part of me wanted to make a run for it, thinking he was some crazy old coot, but the other part wanted to stay and find out what he meant.

"Stick out your wrist," the doc commanded.

"What?" I said, startled once more.

"Stick out your wrist. Your watch is broken, right?"

I did as he asked. His hand moved in one swift motion over my wrist, and before I could question what he was doing, my watch had been completely repaired. I couldn't believe it! The shock from his magic ran up and down my spine. But yes, after the initial jolt, on the side and next to the time adjustor was a small red button, and on the glass casing that previously sheltered the logo now read: Time Waver.

"H-how did you do that?" I stuttered, unable to comprehend.

"I fixed your watch."

I trapped his gaze and I knew he was serious. "What does Time Waver mean?" I wondered, my eyes narrowed. "And what's with this red button?"

"Time Waver is just a name. It holds no importance. But, on the other hand, that red button there is what allows you to travel back in time."

"Go back in ti—"

"Yes, but be warned...every second you go back in time is three minutes that is taken off your life. Use this tool wisely, don't abuse it unless you want to die prematurely." He ended on that ominous note.

I backpedaled. "Wait, so are you saying I'll die if I use this?"

"Everyone dies at some point, Blake. This watch just makes you die sooner... in technical terms."

"Then why would anyone want to use it?"

"I never said you had to. Only use it when you want—or need—to."

Those words rattled me. It felt as though I had all the power in the world but was shackled down. It was like forbidding an eagle from flapping its magnificent wings.

"So how do I use it?" I asked.

"Good question." The doc nodded. "That red button acts like an alarm. The first time you press it, the display screen should reset to 00:00. Adjust the numbers to the exact time you want to travel back. Remember that p.m. and a.m. are relevant. Once you're done, press the button again and it will toss you back in time."

My eyebrows rose instinctively as confusion and suspicion masked my expression.

"For example," Doc Primo continued, "it's about 8:15 right now. If you press the red button and set it to say…6:15, you will travel back to that point in time. Understand?"

I nodded slowly, understanding now. "How far can I go back in time?"

"Seventy-two hours."

This time I nodded. "That's three whole days," I said to myself. Then a fear struck me; if I go back in time, would that mean there will be two of me? I decided to ask.

"No, Blake, there will be no alternate reality. Time is linear, so you're moving on that line back to a previous point." Doc Primo stopped and thought for a moment, probably figuring out a simpler way to explain things. "The watch will transport you to the same exact spot you're in depending on how far you go back."

I tried to wrap my head around the concept. "So you're saying if I press the red button and set it to...let's say...3 hours ago, around 5 a.m., I would be transported into my bed?"

"Precisely, and wearing the same clothes you were wearing at that time."

"Would I know I went back in time?"

He chuckled, obviously enjoying my bewildered state. "Yes, you will retain all knowledge and information from the time and place from which you traveled."

I smiled. I didn't know if I was starting to believe him or not, but the idea of actually going back in time was enough to get my blood racing. "How many times can I use this power?" I said thoughtfully.

Doc Primo gave out a small cough. "As often as you want but the watch takes time to recharge." He paused to gather another breath before continuing, "However far you've gone back in time, it takes the same amount of minutes, hours, or days, before you can use it again."

"Well, what about going forward in time?" I asked Doc Primo greedily.

He shrugged. "That, my friend, is not possible since it hasn't happened yet. This watch only allows you to travel backwards, not forward, which means you can't jump back to the present. You're forced to relive the amount of time you traveled back."

"Oh," I said, a little disappointed.

He looked sympathetic. "It's just a tool, Blake, remember that. Don't overdo it and use the power only when necessary. And just so we're clear, you must not tell anyone you possess this power, otherwise disastrous things might happen." He winked.

"What?" was all I could manage to say.

Doc Primo clapped my shoulder and smiled. "I hope you use it well. And now I must bid you farewell and good fortune on your endeavors."

Without another word, he disappeared behind a corner. Instinctively, I turned to follow, hoping for further explanations, but all I found were the hordes of New York. I shook my head, throwing skepticism to the back of my mind before continuing to Cristo Rey.

The air grew warm as I quickened my pace. Sweat beads rolled down the brink of my forehead to the cusp of my chin by the time the school's doors became visible. I exhaled deeply and wondered if the history test could be finished in thirty minutes.

I decided to take that shot.

My arms wrung the door open and the teacher, Mr. Parker stared from his desk, surprised to see me.

"Sorry Mr. Parker. I woke up late this morning," I said.

He shot me a stern glance but allowed me to take the exam in the remaining time. I thanked him for his generosity before retreating to my desk. I scanned through the test and took a breath of relief. There were no essay questions.

I pulled a pencil out of my backpack and hastily bubbled in the answers to all the easy questions. I took my time with the rest. By this time, everyone else had finished and was quietly chattering away.

For the ones I didn't know, I made "educated guesses" and turned it in a second before the bell rang.

The rest of the morning dragged by. Most of my classes were just electives, after all, a privilege given to seniors. I walked to the cafeteria for lunch, followed by my friends, Pam and Finn. Unfortunately, our class schedules were mixed and matched, the three of us sharing different interests in electives.

"Should I skip out on lunch today and use the money to go shopping?" Pam wondered out loud, whipping her glossy auburn hair behind her. I've known Pam ever since I could remember. We practically grew up side by side, her living down the street and whatnot.

"I don't really see a point. Nothing you can wear will make you look good," Finn joked.

I couldn't help but laugh. Finn was the funniest and the smartest kid in our class, a shoe-in for this year's class clown, or most successful, or probably both. I met him my freshmen year at Cristo Rey. We had the same biology class and somehow became lab partners to my luck. He was always willing to tutor me in everything I didn't know.

I decided on a carton of juice since I wasn't feeling that famished. Beside me, dozens of rickety cafeteria chairs squeaked along the floor as students swarmed the tables. We grabbed an old one in the corner and the daily chatter began.

"You know what's weird?" Pam addressed us. "For the first time in our high school career we don't have any classes together."

"Really? I didn't seem to notice." Finn was obviously joking.

"I mean it. We should have at least taken one elective together." She scowled.

I shrugged. "Its no biggie. Our last year we should take what we enjoy, right? Pam, you always wanted to take anatomy, and Finn here," I nudged him with my hand, "doesn't have a care in the world. Lunch can be our daily time to catch up."

"Did you get a new watch, Blake?" Finn asked curiously. He must've noticed it when I prodded him.

"Uh yeah, yeah. Just got it actually," I stammered.

"Can I see it?"

"Yeah, I guess." I unfastened the watch and handed it to Finn.

He spent a moment examining it. "Time Waver... I've never heard of this brand before. When did you get it?"

Doc Primo's warning of telling others caused me to hesitate. "Actually, it was my dad's old watch and he bought a new one. So he gave it to me," I lied.

Pam peeked over at the watch and then at me before settling her gaze on the watch again, "Well, it suits you, Blake. Makes you look...sophisticated."

I grinned at her as Finn handed the watch back.

The conversation moved to different topics, which consisted of our top college choices and our upcoming graduation. Sounds geeky to be discussing school in school, but what can I say? We were motivated to succeed.

"So when do you guys want to get together to prep for the SATs?" Pam asked.

"Prep?" Finn sounded confused.

Pam rolled her eyes. "Oh forgot, you don't need to study," she sneered.

"Well, that works out for the best. You can focus on helping us instead," I pointed out.

Finn grunted as Pam beamed with satisfaction.

"So just to clarify, we all signed up to take it the same day, right?" I asked.

"Yes, two weeks from today." They nodded together.

I drew in a deep breath. This is what life was, a course of struggles with the ultimate end of proving our worth to society.

The bell sounded in the air. I stood up and threw away the juice container. "Well, I'm heading to class. I'll see you guys later."

"Hold on, I'm heading that way too, remember?" Pam said.

"Let's meet up after school so I can prep you guys," Finn mocked. "Don't bail out on me."

Pam and I walked briskly across the damp grass. She stayed close to my side, close enough where I felt heat radiating off of her.

"So are you ready?" she asked.

I was confused at first. "Ready for what exactly?"

"The SAT's, what else?"

"Not really. I haven't been studying." I admitted.

Pam giggled as we stopped in front of her classroom. She took one step inside before turning. "So, are we on for later then?"

"Yeah, for sure." I nodded.

She gave me a quick smile before disappearing inside the classroom. I turned the corner and headed for the adjacent building.

The rest of the school day and afternoon went by uneventful. I found Pam and Finn at the public library sitting across from each other. I pulled out the seat next to Pam and sat. My fingers grazed along the worn cover of the prep book and from there, the studying for our futures began. Finn breezed through most of the practice questions, managing to get a perfect score, of course. Pam on the other hand, did well enough to warrant a smile breaking across her lips. Her complexion and unwavering focus kept my pencil from moving. If anything, I was more occupied with her than I was with studying. I bit down on my bottom lip, wondering what I was feeling but by the time the library closed at six, I had no answer and felt very unaccomplished.

The journey home was a frustrating one. Not only did I feel stupid but also, I remembered I didn't drive this morning. It was half past six when I arrived at my typical suburban house. A simple one-story, four bedrooms, two bathrooms, and comfortable backyard type of house. I drove my coat off my shoulders before stepping inside. Strolling into the kitchen, I thought of nothing but what was for dinner. My mother, the most hard-working person I knew, was by the oven pulling out tonight's pot roast. Off to the side was my dad, the only Lakers fan in this state, whistling as he prepped the table for dinner.

"Welcome home, Blake," he said.

"I was beginning to get worried. I hope you're hungry," my mom chirped from behind the counter.

I smiled. "Yeah I'm famished, Mom. Studying takes a lot out of me," I breathed in the smell of a home-cooked dinner and fell into bliss.

I dropped my backpack in my room before returning to the dining table with my folks. My mouth filled with saliva as the pot roast invaded my nostrils with its euphoric aroma.

I thanked my mom again before digging in.

After the good dinner, I retreated to my room to start on homework. I figured the earlier I started, the more time I had to review for the SATs. My back stayed crunched over my desk and by the time I felt satisfied with my studying, the numbers on my watch struck midnight. I hadn't realized how late it was. A thought occurred to me to test out Time Waver and continue studying but I quickly brushed that aside—time travel had to be a joke. Exhaustion crept over my body, unnerving my muscles and detaching my mind from reality. I lumbered into bed without a second thought and allowed the darkness to drop under my eyes.

At the sound of chirping birds and the feel of cool breeze coming through the window, I forced myself out of bed. I checked the clock and realized I was up early. I followed my usual routine of showering and eating cereal before stepping out the door. I made a beeline to my unreliable car and climbed into the driver seat. The red paint had rusted beyond repair and the inside dashboard could use a little sprucing. I sank deep into the cushion and drew in a breath before attempting to start the car. The sound of my 1970 Trans-Am coming to life startled me. I knew the engine was a hit or miss, and today seemed to be a good day. After letting the car warm up I threw the lever to Reverse and headed for school. After parking in the student lot, I ventured into school grounds and found a healthy oak tree begging to be leaned upon. I complied naturally, sitting with my back against the trunk. I began contemplating on what to do at that point, but those thoughts led me in a different direction and before I realized it, I was thinking of my future. Pretty soon my mind was swamped with bittersweet thoughts.

I'm in a city that's filled with inspiration. So, why is it that I can't find any? What is my purpose; what am I meant to do with my life? Why do I put up with all this schooling if I'm still in the dark? If only there was a sign to point me in the right direction. It didn't take much for my feelings of gloom to sink deeper as I thought of how untalented and ungifted I really was. Trailing that thought, I began to envy Finn. He was so naturally clever it was just plain unfair to the rest of us. The feeling of envy spurned jealousy and I knew I had to stop. Finn deserved his gifts—he was a good guy, no doubt, and had a lot of heart. Telling myself that over and over again, my gloom soon lifted.

"Well, I shouldn't pity myself, there's still hope for me," I said to myself. "As long as I have free time…I should use it productively…"

I fell deep into my prep book's information and didn't come out of it until something suddenly rustled behind me.

"Wow, studying so early?" Pam giggled as she tousled my hair.

Her gesture, although playful, meant nothing to her but something to me. We were best friends and that was that.

I leaped to my feet and closed the book. "Well, I was up early and there was nothing better to do."

"So, where's Finn?" I asked Pam.

Her eyebrow poked up. "He said he was going to the doctor's today for a check-up, remember?"

I shook my head.

"He told us yesterday when we were studying. You should pay more attention, Blake." Pam rolled her eyes.

Our conversation ended abruptly with the sound of the first period bell. I bade her goodbye at her classroom before marching diligently towards mine.

"Class, please turn in today's homework. Place it in a nice stack on my desk if you will," Mr. Parker instructed as class begun.

I dug through my backpack for the assignment I did last night. Sweat beads dribbled down from the forming crease on my forehead as the seconds ticked by. Did I really forget to put it in my bag?

I dug deeper only to find pieces of lint and an old quarter. I closed my eyes and mentally backtracked my steps. I did this for a moment and then realized I'd left it on my desk. I slumped into my seat, peeking through the slits between my fingers as the rest of the class turned in the twenty-five points I would miss.

"Is that all the papers?" Mr. Parker asked. "Turn it in now or forever hold your peace."

"Only if I remembered to bring it with me. Only if I could go back in time and grab it this morning." I groaned.

Time Waver.

Of course I still had my watch. But how likely is it that Doc Primo actually spoke the truth...? But then again... what did I have to lose?

"Now let me see, what time did I leave for school—7:00?" I asked myself. "Better set it to 6:45 just to make sure..."

I eagerly pressed the red button the side of my watch. The current time disappeared and reset itself to 00:00 just as the Doc said it would.

I held my breath as I adjusted the time to 6:45. I drew in one deep breath and closed my eyes before pressing the button again.

A slight whoosh whisked past my ears and everything around me went hazy. The sensation was comparable to that of a carnival ride—where the rider spins like a dreidel but excluded the nausea effect, which I was thankful for. The next time I opened my eyes, I was sitting at my kitchen counter with the bowl of cereal I had this morning. A smile crept along my lips and I couldn't help but jump in joy because I was certain that I possessed the power of time travel. I laughed all the way to my room and didn't stop until Mr. Parker's assignment was carefully tucked into my backpack. I wondered then if my car would start on the first try like it did this morning.

I twisted the key into the ignition and just like before, the engine came to life. Everything seemed exactly the same. I stopped at the same red lights. Even the cars next to me were the same. This was unbelievable, this was impossible, but more importantly this was magnificent. Who knew my being late to school yesterday would bear such an amazing fruit? Maybe it was fate, or maybe it was karma for helping out Doc Primo. Well, either way, this power was mine and I planned on using it to my advantage.

2
The SATs

IN THE EARLIER more rebellious years of my life, there was only one person who could make me listen. My dad was my mentor ever since I was a kid, and every time a difficult situation presented itself, I turned his advice over in my head.

"Everything happens for a reason son," he lectured me. "Learn from your experiences and grow into a man. No matter what happens, as long as you're alive by the end of the day, then you should have the strength to pick yourself up."

Looking back at those words, I had to give a slight chuckle at his philosophy. Maybe I was being insensitive, maybe I was defying the laws of nature with time traveling, but if there was a reason for this "experience" then it should be taking advantage of the situation. I fought against instinct and excitement to test run Time Waver—so much that it was aching my very bones, but I heeded Doc Primo's advice of not overusing it.

"Hey Blake, what did you get for #34?" Pam asked me helplessly.

I turned away from my thoughts and glared down at the SAT prep book in front of me.

I rubbed my chin thoughtfully. "I think it's B."

"B? Really?" Pam looked doubtful and turned to ask Finn for confirmation. I would've felt hurt if I was sure of my answer, but I wasn't, so of course the ideal route was to go to Finn.

"Yeah it's B all right," he replied casually.

Pam's expression seemed a little surprised that I came up with the right answer but it disappeared just as fast. I shot her a glare but it shifted to interest when she used one hand to play with her hair and the other to hold the book. I had to force myself to look away before the duration of staring became unnatural.

"I can't believe the test is tomorrow!" she freaked. "I am so not prepared for this." My eyes flickered to her again as she looked up from the book.

"You'll do fine, just relax," Finn said as he played with his pencil.

"How do you know that?" she shot back.

"I don't really. I just told you what you wanted to hear." Finn snorted.

My mouth opened to laugh but it stopped short when Pam glowered at me. I jotted down information as Finn and Pam argued about something irrelevant. After a few minutes, I was already exhaling with boredom. I glanced away from Pam, Finn and my prep book and out the window. It was a nice, sunny day. Not the sunny hot kind, but the sunny chilly day, the best weather for any outing. I wasn't much for liking the outdoors, but any alternative was better than studying in the library. We were like test monkeys for society. At the end of the day there is always another test. I exhaled sharply before leaning back in my chair. The public library was littered with kids prepping for the same test. Trish Warner sat with Bill Gavin out by the corner with a dozen of books stacked on their table. Nina Bernard was adjacent to them, her eyes buried deep in the newest edition of prep books.

Everyone seemed so focused and intent on scoring well. Everyone besides Finn, who, on any given day, could fall asleep on the exam and still do better than me. Did I lack the same motivation or work ethic as everyone else? I do want to succeed, but why couldn't I focus on the drive there?

I groaned, frustrated at my lack of resolve.

We stayed at the library till daylight escaped the sky. Everyone was too exhausted to continue, so we called it quits and opted to rest up for the big day tomorrow. Since

Pam and I settled on carpooling with Finn, we could do an emergency study session in the car ride there.

"So, are you getting nervous yet?" Pam asked as I walked her to her car. Finn had found a closer parking spot so he said his goodbyes first. Strangely, I was thankful for that—it sounded mean, but sometimes I did wish Pam and I had more time together alone.

I smiled at her. "Yeah, I feel the butterflies in my stomach already."

"I thought butterflies were only associated with romantic feelings." She giggled playfully.

I guess in that sense, she was partly right. Lately I have been seeing Pam in a different way, a more girlfriend type of way. But there were unspoken rules about dating friends that couldn't be broken, no matter what.

"Fine. I feel wasps in my stomach already." I rolled my eyes. "How's that expression?"

"Weird," she retorted.

I nudged her with my elbow and knocked her off balance. She gasped before retaliating with a punch to my arm. By the time our banter was over, we were next to her car, forcing a quick goodbye.

● ● ●

"Blake! Get up! We're going to be late!"

I woke with a start. Pam was sitting on the foot of my bed looking a little annoyed.

"Come on!" she shrilled.

It took me a moment to adjust to the situation. The first question of relevance was whether I was wearing any pants underneath the covers. I was. And second, why was Pam in my bedroom while I was asleep? But I was too tired to care. I rolled to my side and threw the blanket over my head.

"Finn is going to be here any second," Pam said, this time a little more calmly.

That I was able to register.

I directed Pam to wait for me downstairs before tossing the blanket to the side. Today was the day of reckoning. The day that will decide my future.

I leapt across the room and dug in my wardrobe for something to wear. After pulling on a pair of jeans and a sweatshirt, I searched frantically for socks, pulling one out the drawer and finding another under my bed.

When I finished dressing, I went to the bathroom to freshen up before going downstairs to where my mom was waiting with a glass of orange juice.

"That was delicious, Mrs. Dawson." Pam finished the last sip of her cup.

I had to take huge gulps because, not a second later, a blaring horn deafened the neighborhood.

"Got to go, Mom, I'll see you later." I downed the rest of the juice.

Pam muttered another quick thank you before I dragged her out the door. I grabbed shotgun before

Pam could, and her snarling didn't stop until we were already on the main street.

While Finn meandered through traffic, Pam could be seen through the rearview mirror cramming as best she could. I, on the hand, had given up and decided to go with the flow. Twice at every red light, Pam either complained or asked a question—or, in the most severe case, demanded to tell her what exactly would be on the test.

"Do you think this will be on here?" She pointed at five different sets of problems.

I glanced at each of the problems. "Who knows."

Pam exhaled sharply as Finn stumbled into one of his frequent road rages.

"Man, everyone is driving so slow!" He grumbled. "I should just rear-end every car and teach them a lesson."

I decided not to intervene; instead, I snuggled into my seat and rested my head on the window. My eyes lingered on the outside view until the heat in the car began to make me drowsy. I closed my eyes for the remainder of the trip and didn't open them again until we were at the designated testing area.

I thought Pam, Finn and I were early, but I was dead wrong. There were rows of students huddled in front of a wooden board examining what room they're supposed to be in. I was careful as I squeezed through the masses to the bulletin at the front.

"Can you see what room I'm supposed to be in?" Pam said from behind me. I assumed she couldn't break through the crowd.

I traced the list until I found her name: Pam Wicker. "Yeah, I see you. You're in room 3B."

I found my name a short time afterwards and to my disappointment I was in a different room than Pam and Finn.

I walked with them to room 3B first. Unexpectedly, Finn went up to the glass window and pressed his nose up tightly against it, staring into the empty classroom.

"What are you looking at?" I asked him, trying not to snicker.

"Looking for a seat I like," he replied. I went up to the window and looked through it. All the seats seemed to be identical.

"You wouldn't understand, man," Finn said after I rolled my eyes. "And shouldn't you be getting to your class, Mr. Dawson?"

I shot him a dirty look. "Fine Mr. Evans. I will be taking my leave now." I wished them luck and lumbered away to my classroom: 2A. It was right around the corner so I didn't have to walk far. I found a couple students outside, waiting. I stayed a little ways apart from them, not wanting to strike up any unnecessary conversations. After a moment, the instructor bumbled towards us. He was a fat man, showing just enough neck where it didn't seem like nothing was holding up his giant head. His eyes did a quick sweep over the kids he had to monitor and gave a loud snort. He threw the door open and waddled inside. The kids closest to the door shot each other quick glances before following the fat man inside.

I found a seat next to a pimply kid, who by far, looked the most out of place. He had a skinny figure with a baby face riddled with a bad case of acne. I shuddered as I remembered what it felt like to go through that awkward stage. But to my surprise, he had enough confidence to speak to me, a total stranger.

"Are you nervous?" the boy squeaked.

"Yeah. What about you?"

"Of course. Who isn't?"

After that short exchange of words, we ran out of things to talk about. I spent the remainder of the waiting period watching the kid twitch and shift nervously around in his seat.

"Alright, settle down, settle down," the pudgy instructor addressed us. "Pull out a number two pencil and take a deep breath."

We did as he asked, almost robotically.

"Cheating will not be tolerated, do you understand me?" he said.

Everyone nodded vigorously.

"Okay then." He went down row-by-row passing out the test. I couldn't tell which expression was more apparent, fear or anticipation that was slathered across every kid's face in this room.

"Thanks," I murmured as the instructor handed me the test.

"After you're done bubbling in your name, you may begin." The instructor yawned. "After finishing up the first part, we will take a thirty minute break before continuing. And you can not take the second portion of the test early."

He waddled back to his seat and pulled out today's newspaper. All around me the scratch of pencil against paper resonated through the room as everyone got to work. I bubbled in my name and the rest of my personal information slowly. I was in no rush honestly, and I didn't know why.

I flipped the page to the first question. It was a grammar problem.

My mind sifted back to the lecture on test-taking skills that Finn, Pam, and me attended back at school. If I remembered correctly, I should answer all the easy questions first.

I scanned through the first page and the second. I groaned quietly to myself as I realized there were ten, possibly twelve, questions I knew absolutely. That was bad, statistic-wise. My thoughts were soon swamped with despair and anger. I should've seen this coming. This is what I get for winging all the study sessions.

Maybe I should go back in time and study harder, I thought. I followed that conclusion till it led to a sudden sunshine. I should spend this time memorizing what was going to be on the test, go back in time, study those questions and then take the test.

"Let me think…" I pondered as I glanced quickly around the room at all the pitiful kids who did not possess the same gift as I. How far should I go back?

Every second I go back is three minutes that is taken off my life…so the obvious thing is to not go back to far. But then again, what is death knocking a few days early right? If I'm successful and happy, it shouldn't matter when I die.

No, no, no.

I want to live a long life and experience as much as I can. But, I won't have a life unless I do well on this stupid test.

Wait a minute…I don't have to go back that far.

I remembered this morning Pam had brought her study books with her. That's all I needed really, just a car ride to memorize what would be on the test. I had to fight against the laughter building inside of me as I screamed in glee internally. Pam was my lifesaver and she didn't even know it.

I straightened my back and redirected my focus to the test. I read through the entire test over and over again until I was sure I could recite the questions verbatim. Time was a small price to pay; I wasn't taking a risk with my future.

I glanced down at my watch.

It's been about an hour and thirty since the test started. So if I go back two hours, I should be in Finn's car...

I rubbed my eyes as I pressed the red button on my watch. Just like before, the time reset itself to 00:00. I set the timer to two hours previous and drew in a deep breath. I slapped the red button and the same whoosh of air and haziness swirled around my senses, lifting my feet and planting me exactly where I planned to be.

"Do you think this will be on here?" Pam pointed at the five different sets of problems.

I examined the problems more carefully this time around, "This one since—"

I was cut off as Finn let loose his road rage verbally. He said the exact same thing, word for word. It seems like even if I change my words and possibly actions, it won't have that big of an effect on the continuity of events.

"Hey Pam," I said, my tone light, "can I borrow one of those books?"

I didn't want to just grab the book then, so I waited until she acknowledged my request. I flipped it open to the practice exams and scanned them for similar questions I saw on the real SATs.

"What's gotten into you?" Finn's eyes left the road momentarily to look at me. "You've never been one to do a last minute study session."

I faked a yawn, trying to sound bored. The last thing I wanted was to continue a pointless conversation. "Well, the test is kind of important."

He grunted and looked like he wanted to retort but stopped. I was thankful for his consideration.

I didn't waste another moment since every second had become crucial. I had to strain my memory to recall what I had practiced in verbatim. But I guess now I had a reason to thank the slow drivers that littered today's roads because by the time I stepped out of Finn's car for the second time today, I was confident.

Forgetting that Finn and Pam needed to know what their assigned room was, I almost breezed past everyone before being reminded.

"Can you check for me, Blake?" Pam pleaded. "I can't see over all these people."

I pretended to look over everyone's heads for a second before reporting back to her. "You and Finn are in the same room—3B."

I decided to stick to what I did this morning, feeling that if I deviated too much away from natural events, things might end up different than I planned. So just like before, I accompanied them to their room, loitered around before being scolded by Finn to leave.

I grabbed the same seat and waited for the pimply kid to start a conversation with me like he did last time.

"Are you nervous?" He squeaked the same way as before.

"Not really," I said, truthfully.

He looked shocked. "How is that possible?"
"I'm just not."

I breezed through the first part of the test with ease. I calculated in my head, there were maybe one or two I didn't know precisely. I had to control my delight as I waited for the rest of my peers to finish before going on break. I spent most of the time contemplating what situations would permit time travel and what wouldn't. My mind wrapped around possible scenarios and the end result was always the same—that I will only use this power to further my percent of success in this lifetime. Once we were allowed a leave for break, I paraded around the area until Pam and Finn came out. Finn looked confident as usual, and as for Pam...not so much.

"How was it?" I asked them, raising both eyebrows.
"It was fine," Finn answered first. Pam's lips pouted out as they always did when she didn't know how to respond.
"I guess it was okay," she finally muttered.
"Hopefully," I said. "We all do well."
"That's a no-brainer," Pam snapped at me. "No matter what happens, you and Finn promise to go to the best school you can get into, okay?" She paused to suck in a quick breath, "And no matter what, we're going to keep in touch, right?" She ended on a stern tone.
I didn't doubt this because I knew even if we went to separate schools, it only meant our physical bodies were

separated. With today's technological advances, keeping in touch is a breeze.

The break sounded long on paper but was actually short in real-time. Without a moment's hesitation, I murmured goodbye to Finn and Pam, and returned to classroom 2A.

There was a shuffle next to me as the pimply kid took his seat. "How did you do on the first part?" he squeaked from behind his calculator.

"I think I did alright." I gave a slight shrug. "You?"

"Not so great."

"Why's that?"

He groaned so loud that it startled me. "Because I guessed on like half the problems!"

"Well, there's a second part. Maybe you'll do better on this one," I said.

He snarled quietly and our conversation ended there.

"Okay, let's get this over with," the pudgy instructor muttered. "Once you're done with the test, bring it to my desk and leave. *Capiche*?"

Everyone nodded again.

"Alright, then. Proceed."

I stared down at my desk. There were three objects on it: the test, my pencil, and my calculator. I picked up the pencil first and flipped open the test to the second part. The veins in my arm tensed as I began solving the equations with ease. Most of the time, I didn't have to use my calculator, but I did once it was time to double-check my work. Just to be on the safe side, and with so much time remaining, I triple-checked my answers. Once I felt confident enough to bid the SATs farewell, I stood from my desk, shuffled past the full classroom, and placed my exam on the instructor's desk. I would've smiled at him if he bothered to look up from his newspaper but he didn't, so I turned and headed for the door.

As I walked down the row, everyone's eyes bored into me. I had to wonder if it was because I finished the exam so fast. I chuckled to myself as I threw the door open and walked out to the sun beaming across the horizon.

3
Unfair Advantage

WITH NOTHING BUT the future to look forward to, the months passed by like the secondhand on a clock. Each week was like a tick, counting down till the day the results came back.

"When are our scores supposed to come in again?" Pam asked at lunch one day.

"Soon I believe." Finn nodded. "Are you still nervous about your results? It's been months since we took it."

Pam's lips pouted out. "I'm not naturally smart like you, Finn, so I have a right to be nervous…isn't that right, Blake?"

"Right," I responded quickly and then took a bite of my sandwich.

Suddenly but not surprisingly, the silent bug landed on everyone's lips and clamped down. No one knew what else to talk about, so instead, we drowned the

silence with the sound of nibbling on our barely clas-
sifiable lunch.

"So Blake..." Finn said suddenly. I glanced up to find a
weird expression smacked on his face. "You've been acing
every test lately...I don't want to sound like a jerk or anything, but I'm kind of surprised."

"What do you mean?" I feigned confusion.

"We all know," Pam interjected and my eyes fell on her.
"That you were never one to take studying seriously. So
what happened?"

I scratched the back of my head, my eyes lingering on
hers. At that moment, I wanted to spill everything but I
couldn't. Although they were my closest friends, this was
something I can never share with them. The truth was that
I've been using this power quite generously the past few
months. I knew I shouldn't have...but it's been addicting.
I was now rolling around with top-notch grades, so who
could complain with that? Sure, my life is being cut down
slowly, but that's a price I'm willing to pay in order to be
successful.

"I don't know. I guess it just hit me that we're going to
be out of here soon. And my parents are going to kill me
if I don't get into a good school, you know? I finally realized I had to buckle down and get my priorities straight,"
I lied smoothly.

I exhaled easily once it looked like they believed me.

The class bell rang exactly a minute after the conversation ended. I got up and threw the remainder of

my lunch in the trash bin. As usual, I walked Pam to class before heading to my own. It was only a photography elective so the second I climbed into my seat my eyes drooped. My nap didn't last long; an annoying tap on my shoulder confiscated whatever drowsiness I had. I looked over my shoulder and found Amber Stone to be the source of annoyance. She curled her fingers away as soon as my eyes ran over her.

"Yeah?" I asked when she didn't say anything.

Her face reddened with intensity and she bit down on her bottom lip. Amber Stone was a cheerleader, one of the popular kids. I couldn't help but wonder why she would talk to someone like me. I didn't consider myself a loser but I didn't consider myself cool either.

I stared at Amber's complexion, watching her with unnatural attention as her rosy lips parted. "I was wondering if you could be my math tutor," she said, a little shy.

"Really? You want me to be your tutor?"

"Yeah, you've been getting A's lately. So how about it?"

It was impossible to respond faster than I did. "Sure!"

Her face lit up and a smile stretched from one side of her cheek to the other. "Okay, how about we get together this Friday after school?"

I nodded.

Amber skipped away, her long blonde hair resting on her lower back. I fidgeted throughout class, pondering what her words meant. Amber wasn't dumb, she was the type to use her sea green eyes to get what she desired.

And if that failed, her dreamy voice was perfect for pity grades. If that wasn't the case then is it a date? Or did she really need help with calculus? Either way, it didn't matter...I was going to see one of the most popular girls in school this weekend.

• • •

On Friday, I was a nervous wreck, to say the very least. School flew by and before I had the time to glance at my watch again, I was standing in front of Amber's house. I rang her doorbell twice and slowly curled my finger back into the insides of my pocket. A moment later, the door swung open and Amber led me into her room.

I sat on her bed and stared around.

"I'll go get some sodas. I'll be right back." She flashed me a quick smile before leaving me alone in her room. Everything was tidy and perfect—no clothes lied on the floor, no trash to be picked up, and no strange odors. Pictures on the large dresser next to the desk, caught my attention and I moved a step in that direction. They were childhood memories caught in frames of her and Cory Wraith.

That's right... last time I checked, she was dating him.

I drove that thought to the recesses of my mind as I examined her trophy shelf. From outside the room came the sound of footsteps so I immediately resigned from snooping. Amber waltzed in carrying two cans of soda.

"So what do you need help on?" I asked.

She looked thoughtful for a moment. "Whatever we're learning now."

"Have you not been going to class?" I joked. "It's pretty straightforward."

"I'm sorry I'm not smart like you," she said, a little curt.

I laughed gently. "Maybe we should get started then!"

The rest of the day flew by, but it didn't end there, or at least, I wouldn't let it. By nightfall our stomachs were growling, so we left her house. I offered to drive, so we climbed into my Trans-Am and zoomed off. We stopped at an old burger joint, not one of the mainstream chains, but a family-owned place with friendly lights and people.

I ordered a burger and fries and she got hash browns with a milkshake. As we sat down to eat, there was a moment of stillness between us. An uncomfortable silence, one I wanted to break with the one zinging question bubbling inside of me: were we on a date? I had finished half my burger when she started the conversation.

"Excuse me, sir, but you have been ignoring me all night."

"Oh my sincerest apologies. I didn't know I was supposed to be entertaining you." I played along, and then smiled. Her lips pouted.

Before another uncomfortable silence settled in, I decided to voice the question I'd been dying to ask the whole night.

Her expression didn't display surprise. I assumed that was a good sign.

"On a date?" Amber teased as she took a sip from her milkshake. "What do you think?"

I swallowed loudly. "What about Cory? Last time I checked, you guys were still dating." I paused to gauge her reaction before continuing, "Or did you just break up, and now I'm just some sort of rebound." I finished there.

She giggled, taking me by surprise. "The truth, Blake, is that I've always thought you were cute. I got tired of waiting for you to ask me out so I did it instead."

"So you and—"

"You don't have to worry about that. It's finished." She reassured me.

My stomach settled as those words rang in my ears. Was it possible that an average kid like me was capable of dating a girl like Amber? Whatever the case, I should just enjoy the ride for what it's worth, because let's face it, how often do guys like me get this type of chance?

Once we were done eating, we walked outside to the lot, her head resting on my shoulder. Suddenly, rain came down so we hurried to my car, listening to the water dink against the metal roof. Amber was sniveling beside me so I turned the key and flashed the heater. I pushed all the vents towards her in an effort to seem chivalrous.

"So, what do you want to do now?" I asked. "Then again...there's not much to do if it's raining this hard."

She turned towards me and smiled. She curled up into her jacket and for some reason looked alarmingly shy.

"How about we just cruise around town and talk?" I suggested.

She didn't object, so we zoomed off.

It was still very cold inside the car. I didn't know why since the heaters were blasting, but nevertheless Amber was still shivering beside me. To get her mind off the blistering cold, I asked her questions about her family, school, and cheerleading. The last topic set her into a frenzy. I had no idea Amber was so passionate about it until I brought it up. In turn, she pushed the spotlight on me and we discussed what my interests were. I couldn't tell her all I did was hang out with Pam and Finn, so I lied.

"I play basketball when I have spare time." I said.

"Really?" Amber sounded surprised. "Why don't you try out for the school team?"

I gulped. "That's a big commitment, and it's just for fun I mean, going to a local park, meeting strangers and playing against them. That's what I like most about the sport."

"Ah I see." Her lips parted.

I took exception to that. Amber's lips enticed my gaze, and it didn't help that when it felt chapped, she would apply her lip-gloss in a suggestive manner.

It wasn't long before midnight crept along that I reluctantly called it a night since she had curfew. We continued the conversation for most of the trip back home. I brought up cheerleading again and as she talked, her lips moved, curving upwards especially when discussing her intentions to continue that passion in college.

I found parking on the side of her street and cut the engine. The heater had warmed the car enough to stop Amber's shivering, which I was thankful for. I wrenched my door open and blew hot air into my hands before attending to her. I flew around the car and pulled the passenger door open. As I walked her to the front steps of her house, the chilly wind whipped our faces. It wasn't until we were at her door that we muttered our goodbyes.

"So I'll see you around sometime?" was all I managed to say.

Amber looked disappointed but cleaned up her expression before I commented on it. "Yeah. Have a good night, Blake." She smiled again.

I turned and walked away in utter disgust with myself. I climbed into my car in a fit of rage and slammed my hands against the steering wheel.

See you around sometime?

Come on, any other line would've been better than that one. And why didn't I kiss her goodnight? She wanted it. I wanted it. Then why couldn't I make it happen?

I sighed out loud. Next time I would definitely kiss her.

No, I should kiss her now.

I eagerly pulled out Time Waver and set the time to five minutes previous. The reality around me twirled in a circular motion, lifting my feet as the force pulled my body into the magical tornado, and thrusting me back five minutes in time. I found myself standing outside her car door again. I repeated my actions and walked her to the house.

"Did you have fun?" I grinned seductively.

"Of course," she replied.

"Well, so do you really want to end tonight like this?"

She giggled. "I don't know, how would you end it?"

That was the cue.

I curled one arm around her waist and pulled her body closer. I closed my eyes and found her lips pressing against mine. It was a fact that my physical body was kissing Amber, but for some reason, my mind was picturing Pam. The latter name made my head swirl with bliss and those few long seconds were the best seconds of this entire year.

I released her waist after kissing her and bade her goodnight. I walked away and drove home feeling confused and guilty.

The next day, I stayed in bed past noon, despite being awake for some time. I spent the minutes and hours replaying the kiss in my head and wondered what Amber thought. What would she say if I told her I was picturing someone else? Or was it just simple fun for her too? My thoughts were soon disrupted as my mom's voice crashed into my room.

"Blake, the mail is here!"

My dad must've forgotten to take it in before going to work. I groaned before leaping out of bed to make my way towards the mailbox. I pulled out several items: a postcard from my aunt and uncle in Hawaii, some bills, and a large white envelope that was addressed to me.

I didn't think much of it as I placed everything else on the dining table. I carried the envelope up to my room and threw it on the desk before lying back down and resting my eyes.

The feeling of drowsiness almost overcame me until the ringing of my cell phone demanded my attention. I fished for it with closed eyes before realizing it was foolish. I exhaled heavily as I climbed out of bed to search. I found it in my pants pocket and checked the name of the person calling me.

It was Pam. I eagerly flipped the phone open and said hello a little breathlessly.

"Did you check your SAT results yet?" she replied, also a little out of breath. "They came in today!"

"No, I don't remember..." I trailed off as I realized the envelope addressed to me was the results. "Oh, I do have it. Never mind!"

"So, how did you do?"

"I don't know, I haven't checked yet."

She scowled. "Then check right now!"

"Okay, okay. Hold on." I switched the phone to speaker mode and dropped it on my bed. I glided to my table and grabbed the envelope. I twirled it in my hands a few times as moisture worked its way down my nose. I turned the envelope over, my hands shaking unnaturally. I found the spot where I'm supposed to tear but my fingers stopped for no particular reason.

"Blake? Blake?" Pam pressed. "Are you there?"

I hurried back to my phone, my hands unwilling to open the envelope.

"I don't hear any ripping," she muttered. "What's taking you?"

"Hold on!" I snapped.

I took a few deep breaths before tearing the envelope like a wild animal. I found a piece of a paper inside, pulled it out and scanned it. I skipped over the beginning paragraphs and searched for my results.

It was near the bottom in big block numbers. I calculated quickly in my head to figure out my total score. 2350.

"I don't hear anything. You did bad, huh?" Pam sneered.

She was joking but a part of me actually did want that. How would she feel once I told her I got a near-perfect score? I held the letter and glanced at the results every few seconds, just to make sure I did the math correctly. After I was over the initial shock, I told Pam my score as smoothly as possible, explaining to her it was most likely luck that got the results.

"A-a-amazing, Blake!" She gasped. "I'm so proud of you! I only managed to get a 2130."

I sighed, knowing that she was disappointed with her score. I couldn't say anything at this point, but then again, what was there to say: I'm sorry for doing better than you?

After a moment of silence, Pam said, "Uh, I'm going to call Finn now and ask him what he got."

"You didn't ask him yet?" I responded, my voice a little shaky.

"Nope. Not yet. I wanted to see what you got first."

"Okay, we'll talk later."

She hung up and I fell back on my bed. I read the letter over and over again as a bittersweet feeling sank into the pit of my stomach. Of course, having a near perfect score on the SAT was great, but I'd cheated.

A knock came on my door and I sat up.

"So what did you get, Blake?" my mom asked. I smiled and handed her the letter. Her face went from rosy to pale in an instant. "Oh dear! Oh my goodness, Blake!"

I rolled my eyes, assuming that if she reacted this way she didn't expect much of me. "When did you—I mean, how did you pull this off?"

I was dead on. It was almost as if my own mom accused me of cheating. I shrugged. "I don't know…luck?"

"We should celebrate today!" She burst with joy. "Do you want to go out to dinner or do you want me to cook your favorite meal?"

"Really, Mom, it's fine. It's not that big of a deal."

"Don't be modest now, Blake."

"Really, Mom, it's alright. I'm calling Finn now to ask him what he got."

That was the cue for my mom's exit and she got the hint. But she couldn't leave before proudly kissing my forehead. I found my phone and texted Finn.

It was only a matter of seconds before Finn texted back. "2350. I heard you got the same?"

I texted back saying yes.

The rest of the day followed in the same manner as the first ten minutes of opening the envelope. My dad was overly ecstatic, even more so than my mom. That evening we decided to eat out. My dad did something he'd never done before: he invited everyone in the family—cousins, aunts, and uncles, the whole shebang.

"So, how's all the attention treating you?" my dad asked the moment we returned home from dinner.

"I love it, Dad. Can't possibly live without it!" I said, sarcastically.

"Aw, don't be like that, son. Everyone in the family was just showing you how proud they are."

"Yeah, well, all the attention has drained me," I muttered. "I'm going to bed."

I raced to my room and closed the door gently. I sat on the bed and stared into space. Monday was coming up, and school was a perfect scenario for information sharing and receiving. If I thought my family was bad, my classmates would be worse. I was now the average kid who got a freakishly good score on the SAT. I sighed and stretched out on the bed.

By the end of the weekend, everyone was still on cloud nine, excluding me. My mom was busy chirping about Ivy League schools and my dad grunted along. Meanwhile, I was sitting at the kitchen counter, poking my eggs with my fork as I thought about the possibilities I had now. There was a singe of guilt bubbling inside my stomach but I fought it down quite easily. After a minute or so, I cleaned off my food with one swift motion and dropped the dish in the sink. I straightened up, took a deep breath, clutched my backpack, and headed for school.

The lunch bell couldn't ring fast enough that day. Once the blissful sound erupted in my ear, I hurried away from everyone and curled into my seat at the usual lunch table. It didn't take long for Finn and Pam to join me.

"You're not going to eat anything?" Pam asked. It was obvious the question was posed for me since Finn was clutching a yogurt container but I chose not to respond.

I felt a hard jab to the side of my chest and I leapt into the air. "What was that for?" I glared at her.

"For ignoring me. What else?" She pulled out a chair and sat.

"So everyone in our class has been talking about you." Finn fought back a laugh.

I shuffled miserably in my seat. Yeah, Finn was dead on. Since first period, I couldn't go ten seconds without hearing someone whisper my name or plain ask me to confirm my score. If their tone was more envious or accepting then I would've felt flattered, but their choice of words and tone alerted me to their true feelings. Suspicion and judgment.

"Well, things will blow over soon," Finn reminded me cheerfully as he ate a spoonful of yogurt. "We still have prom and graduation coming up."

A minute later I suddenly felt a sharp pain on the side of my head. I didn't have time to react to the sudden blow because at that moment a pair of hands seized my shoulders and threw me to the floor. The sudden impact sent me into a daze. I struggled to stand up. Standing over me was Cory Wraith, a big brute of a kid with very sadistic tendencies.

"What was that for?" I backed up as he inched closer. My eyes flickered around me. I was the center of attention again. All eyes were glued to this run-of-the-mill high school scene.

"WHAT WAS THAT FOR?" His voice shook with anger as he threw off Finn's feeble attempt to hold him back. "HOW ABOUT THE FACT THAT YOU TOOK MY GIRLFRIEND OUT ON A DATE?"

My mind sifted back to Amber Stone. She told me she was recently single. Why the hell would she lie to me?

I wasn't able to trail that thought far enough to reach a conclusion because his fist crashed into my face. I toppled over, the pain ringing in my head intensified with every passing second. I hoped that strike was the end, but the barrage was just starting. He climbed on top of me and bashed every visible part of my body. I managed to cover most of my head but the sudden jolts of pain had me whimpering.

The crowd jeered for me to fight back. Didn't matter what I did. Even if I fought Cory, the results would still be the same. More blows to my stomach sent the wind out through my mouth and I fought to grasp air. But for that split second my mouth was exposed, a fist came into direct contact into it. My head snapped back towards the cafeteria floor as my body went into a sudden numb state. I hoped desperately for the blackness to overtake me—

"Hey! Hey! What are you doing?"

It took a few teachers and staff members to pull Cory off of me, and more to drag him away. I saw the doors slam shut as I bent over to spit out the warm blood. Cory's curses and yelling attacked the thin walls, bouncing around the room. A circle of bodies surrounded me and the haze from the battle blinded me from their faces. The only one I was able to fully make out was Pam crouching over me, tears streaming down her milky skin and wetting my bloody shirt.

4
Top Pick

THE NURSE'S HANDS held me down on the infirmary's bed. I tried jerking away but it was useless, my mind was drained and my body beaten—pun intended.

"I'm fine," I slurred rather stupidly.

The door swung open and Finn and Pam raced in. The latter person dived in front of the nurse and threw my hand into hers. Finn stood in the back, arms crossed with a disgruntled expression.

"Are you okay?" Pam repeated over and over again. "You look awful."

I struggled to smile at her. "I'm fine Pam, don't worry about me. Look at Finn over there, what's up with him?" I tried to laugh but my bruised ribs kept me from it.

"Stop fidgeting so much. Here, put this over his eye." The school nurse handed Pam an ice pack and she threw it on my forehead.

"I'm sorry Blake. I should've had your back...but it all happened so fast," Finn piped up from the door.

His guilt warmed my insides and made me feel instantly better. Finn was apologizing for not jumping into the fight, full-knowing that if he did, it would've gone on his record.

"It's okay. I didn't react either. You can probably tell by looking at me, can't you?"

A grin crept on the edge of his lips and with a small laugh from Pam, his smirk burst into a full smile.

"Wait a minute," the nurse chirped. "What are you two doing here? Go back to class. Shoo! Shoo!"

Pam scowled and handed me the ice pack. I applied it to my swollen cheek as she stood up and strode over to where Finn was standing. The thumping pain abated a bit so I turned and stood up. I staggered over to them and thanked them for visiting me.

"Blake, get back on the bed!" the nurse squeaked.

I waited for Finn and Pam to squeeze their way out the door before retreating back to the bed. I grabbed a pillow and smothered my face. I peeked from underneath, saw the nurse behind her desk, scribbling paperwork. I felt useless lying around. What's worse is the whole school was talking about me, talking about how I didn't put up a fight and how one-sided my ass kicking was. I grumbled to myself, thinking that in their eyes, I wasn't just the freaky genius who blossomed but now I was Cory Wraith's punching bag.

But wait...I can change what happened.

I can make it so I come out victorious. I had promised myself that I would use my power more discreetly, but another couple hours off my life is nothing compared to the walk of shame I would face tomorrow.

I snorted gleefully as I pictured myself standing over Cory Wraith's body.

"Is something the matter over there?" the nurse called over her shoulder.

"Nope, everything is fine." I hid my happiness. I tried to sound normal but my voice came out all funny and raspy.

"Alright, you can lie down for a bit longer and then you can return to class with the ice-pack."

"You do know best," I whispered as I set Time Waver to the beginning of lunchtime. I closed my eyes and swiped the red button. The air whisked past my body, lifted my legs and planted them at the lunch table next to Finn and Pam.

"...So everyone in our class has been talking about you," Finn said.

I spent a moment figuring out where we were in the conversation. But it was a good thing humans were visual creatures because Finn dipped his spoon into the yogurt he was having for lunch.

"Well, things will blow over soon." He swallowed. "We still have prom and graduation coming up."

Bingo. Those were the last words I heard before getting assaulted.

I glanced behind me and out of the corner of my eye I saw a figure hurrying toward me.

"Right on time," I mouthed.

I kept my glance fixated on him even as he pulled his hand back to form a fist. Before the blow could connect, I swerved my head to the side. His fist connected with the table instead. Pam yelped in surprise but I was way ahead of her. I wrapped my hand around the back of Cory's neck and yanked his head down against the table. The force of the blow wobbled his legs. When he straightened up, his eyes were disoriented and unfocused.

I scoffed to myself, never realizing that the art of surprise was so important. I clenched my right fist and punched him between his eyes.

A crack resonated off his nose; his body slammed into the ground. My eyes danced around the room, catching everyone's surprise and feeding off it.

Yes people, someone like me was able to take down Cory Wraith.

I looked down again on the once-fierce face and saw the pain in his eyes. But I didn't care—I gave him one more swift kick to the ribs before picking up my backpack and leaving the cafeteria. A rush of satisfaction hit me the second I left the room. The adrenaline pumped through my veins, fueling me with desire to pound Cory even more.

Pam and Finn followed shortly after, their expressions a combination of confusion and awe. I tried to play my face off nonchalantly but failed—the rush was just too much to control.

"What the hell happened in there?" Finn thundered. "You just took down Cory Wraith, man. You're insane!"

I scratched my nose and chuckled.

"What are you saying?" Pam said, shocked. "Don't encourage him, Finn!"

I was taken aback. "What do you mean?" I barked.

Her eyes fell short of mine. The awe in them had evaporated and its residue was disappointment.

"Are you going to tell me?" I asked again, this time a bit nicer.

"I don't think you should go around beating people up," she finally said.

"But Blake didn't start it, Cory just went up and tried to hit him!" Finn countered.

"Still... Never mind, you guys don't get it."

"Get what?"

This time her eyes leveled with mine. "You don't think you went a little too far, Blake?" Her words flowed out in a rush. "You don't think that splitting his nose open is a little much? I mean sure, he did attack you, but couldn't you have been the better man and step away? Whatever happened to you taking the high road every time someone has a problem with you? You were never like this before, so why now?"

I couldn't respond. Even if I did, it wouldn't make the situation any better.

Maybe I did go a little too far...but if only she could see what he could've done to me, then she would be singing a different tune.

"What's done is done. I can't change what happened," I said darkly.

Finn gave me a pat on the back and winked. "I think what you did was completely justified."

Pam rolled her eyes and walked away, alone.

The next day was full of excited chatter, as expected. People swarmed me with questions, asking how I took down Cory Wraith. I didn't bother twisting the story, I told them the honest truth: I "saw" him coming and prepared accordingly. But the relentless questions were the least of my worries—Pam, Finn and I intended to go over the list of colleges we planned to apply to. The ideal scenario would be if we all went to the same one, but with the SAT scores that Finn and I had...it looked pretty bleak for Pam to go with us. But there was some good news: by the time all of us got together, Pam had forgiven me for kicking Cory's ass. Finn, on the other hand, couldn't let it go, droning on about the newfound respect he had for me.

"I don't care what college I'm going to. I'm going to succeed anyways," Finn said arrogantly after Pam lectured him about what the "good" schools were.

She made a face before turning to me. "And you, Blake? Where are you planning on going?"

I scratched my chin. "I don't really care, to tell you the truth."

"Not you too..."

I caught Finn's eye and we both laughed. "Well, we should go to a school that's near yours right?" I said.

"No! You have to go to the best school you possibly can!" Pam gasped. "I thought we already agreed on this."

Finn's eyebrows furrowed. "What if we never see you?"

"That's what webcams and cell phones are for."

"I guess," Finn said, defeated.

The following days we did just that. I applied to the top ranked schools in the east and west coast, hoping that at least one would take me. My grades were mediocre freshmen through junior year. But hopefully, my senior grades and SAT score would shed better light on my potential.

"So when do we receive our acceptance letters again?" I brought up the topic a month after applications were due. Finn obviously had no clue, but Pam pulled out her planner and flipped through it.

"Let's see... What's today?"

"April third," Finn and I replied in unison.

"I'd say another week or so."

That was the longest week of my life. School was a drag but at least I was at the top of the academic heap. My love life on the flipside, had hit rock bottom. It couldn't be helped that after my little encounter with Cory, Amber Stone began acting like I didn't exist.

I could only assume she still cared for him and decided to reverse the break-up. It didn't affect my mood that much. I didn't care for her like I did with Pam. I sighed deeply, stuffing my face in my pillow, too lazy to do anything.

"BLAKE!" My mom's voice boomed from the kitchen.

"What is it?" I called back.

"YOUR ADMISSION LETTERS ARE HERE!"

I jumped up from my bed and dashed to the kitchen. My mom stood there with a pile of unopened letters in her hands. I went over to grab them from her shaking hands before taking a peek at the calendar.

"Pam was right, exactly a week... Maybe she has a watch that can travel forward in time..." I mused.

"Open them right here!" My mom clasped her hands together.

"I don't know if I should. I kind of want some privacy, Mom." I ran my fingers through my hair.

"No, do it right here," she commanded.

I drew a breath and did as instructed. I tore the letters open on by one, reading each and every single admission letter word for word. Every time I was done with one, my mother piped up and asked if I got in or not.

And the answer was always yes.

"Even Brown?" my mom squeaked.

I controlled my excitement. "Yes, Mom, even Brown." I tried to sound nonchalant.

But my mom didn't care; she gave a gasp of joy and threw her arms around me. "This is just wonderful, Blake! First person in our family to go to an Ivy League school!"

I stretched out my hand and patted her on the back. "Mom, you're suffocating me...and I haven't decided which school I want to go to yet."

"Oh, right." She sat on the kitchen stool. "Well, whatever you decide, your father and I can pay for most of your tuition. You probably want to dorm too, and food and books...well, you just leave that to us."

I smiled broadly. "I'll probably take a job or something and help you guys out."

Her voice grew stern. "No!" She shushed me. "You focus on school and get a good education. You can support us later when you have a job."

I didn't feel like arguing so I stopped there, fully knowing that my parents wouldn't be able to pay for everything. I should get a part-time job or at least pull out a loan. I gave a sigh and lumbered back to my room. It was a good thing I was accepted to every school I applied to, but it just made my decision that much more complicated. It was difficult to narrow down universities, especially when all of them were great in their own regard. To top it off, I couldn't be more indecisive about my major.

Instead of deciding right there and then, and keeping the conversations short and to the point, I called Pam and asked what school she preferred to go to, figuring that asking her first would make me sound like less of a braggart. She sounded a little disappointed when announcing her plans on attending UCLA the following fall. Finn is definitely the polar opposite of Pam. He just doesn't care about anything: choosing which school to attend, what major he should take, it seemed like his future wasn't a big priority at all.

"What about Brown? It looks pretty good." I suggested.

"Yeah, it does." He sounded bored. "What majors are they known for?"

That remark acted as a fire that ignited all the questions simmering in my head. What major should I go for? Or should I just be undecided now and explore a little? After a few long minutes, Finn brought me back to reality. "Uh Blake, you still there?"

"Yeah, sorry I was busy thinking about your question. I really don't know what majors are good there but I think I'm staying undecided for the time being. You know, explore a little here and there and see what I like."

"Sounds good." Finn yawned.

"But yeah, Brown has a pretty good reputation. I think we'll meet the right people there and plus I heard the girls were pretty hot." I tried my best to sell the idea of going to Brown.

"Yeah, alright. Why not? Its only college, right?"

I threw my fist in the air to demonstrate my victory.

"So what about Pam? What school is she going to?" Finn asked, but at that moment, my dad strolled into my room, face beaming with excitement.

"I got to go, my dad's here," I whispered.

"Alright, I'll give Pam a call myself." He hung up.

I dropped the phone on my lap and waited for my dad to approach me. He sat on the foot of my bed. "So, I heard you got into all the schools you applied to." He grunted. "You must be happy, eh?"

"Not really, so much for narrowing down the list," I retorted.

His eyebrows furrowed and his voice dropped a pitch lower than normal, "Blake, don't let this get to your head. The second you start to think you're better than everyone else is the moment you start to lose those around you." He lectured me.

I didn't understand the point since it was irrelevant to the topic at hand, but I nodded along to avoid a continued lesson.

"Do you have a school in mind?" my dad asked, his tone returning to normal, but he looked suddenly anxious.

"Probably Brown," I said casually.

"Staying in the East Coast, huh? Sure you don't want to go someplace warmer?"

I threw a look outside the window. "No, I like the cold weather. So yeah, preferably the East Coast."

He stared at me for a few seconds and then shrugged. "I guess if that's what you want to do then I can't stop you."

"What do you mean?" I asked, confused. "You don't want me to go to an Ivy League school?"

"It's not that," he said. "I just got off the phone with Pam's mom and she told me Pam was planning on attending UCLA."

"Yeah, she told me already."

"I figured you would want to go to a school closer to her."

I shook my head and my voice came out surprisingly fuzzy. "I'm just trying to think about my future, Dad. Girls can come later."

His expression showed a little disappointment but it was wiped away quickly. "It's good to have ambition in school but don't forget that your life consists of more than just a good job and money. I just want you to be happy, son."

Two life lessons in one day—I wondered what could have spurred this on. But just like earlier, I nodded along, faking acknowledgment to whatever he was saying.

At that moment something painful pierced the side of my chest a little ways below my heart. My teeth gritted against the sudden pain, I couldn't let my dad know there was something wrong with me.

But what was wrong?

The second wave of pain was stronger than the first. It forced my mouth open in shock, but luckily no audible signs of agony escaped my throat. I clamped down on my jaw and spoke through clenched teeth. "Hey Dad, I'm actually kind of tired." I paused for a second to control my breathing. "Can we talk later? I want to lay down for a bit."

He looked at me kind of bewildered but agreed to my request. "Okay, I'll see you later for dinner." He hesitated and then left, closing the door behind him.

I dropped to the floor, clutching the side of my chest. The experience was unlike anything I've ever felt before, it felt like a white-hot knife had splintered into my side and began twisting and slicing its way through. I curled into a ball, thinking the torture would never cease, but in a flash, the pain disappeared.

I sat up and inhaled a couple deep breaths. Usually pain should decrease gradually not disappear in a hurry. Still breathing in gasps, I sat back on my bed and planted my face in my palms.

One single thought ran through my mind. I was using Time Waver too frequently. I should space it out more and decrease its toll on my body. Yes, that was the right thing to do. I don't have to ace everything, just the important stuff.

After reaching that conclusion, another thought entered my mind. Was that what it felt like to die? Flashes of pain that recede once you enter blackness? My life couldn't be slipping away from me already; maybe it would be smart to see a doctor. No. I couldn't worry my parents with that, and I especially wouldn't want to be some paranormal medical case.

I exhaled heavily, yearning to find Doc Primo and ask hundreds of questions. But he would be difficult to find, and I wouldn't know where to begin looking. It was depressing to know he was magic, an illusion I will never grasp even if I had countless years to try. I shook my head out of frustration. I looked at myself in the mirror. Passion blazed in my eyes, and I was pleased with this expression. Time Waver wasn't a burden that brought death closer; no...it was a tool that would bring my dreams to reality.

"What's a few heart-stopping attacks here and there?" I asked myself, laughter dancing along the bridge of my lips.

5
High School Dreams

I WOKE WITH a start the following morning. Although it was barely daybreak, I couldn't keep my eyes shut any more. For some strange reason, I wasn't exhausted. In fact, it was the opposite, I felt energetic.

"Yesterday's heart attack wasn't so bad." I reassured myself. "I just have to be more careful when I travel back. I just need more time for my body to rest." My mood rose as I danced circles to the bathroom, pausing once to exhale at the rising sun.

After washing up and changing out of my pjs, I skipped down to the kitchen to pour myself a glass of orange juice and butter some toast. Sitting there in complete solitude, and munching on my breakfast somehow got my mind racing for the upcoming festivities.

And by that I meant prom.

I yawned loudly, threw the dish in the sink, and stretched. "Who am I going to ask to prom?" I wondered out loud. "It's only a couple weeks away. If I wait any longer, all the good dates will be taken."

I turned over possible girls in my head. After realizing that most of them already had a significant other, my sunshine mood faded to moonlight and I stood there with a frown on my face. I lumbered back to bed to lie down. I threw my arm over my eyes and pulled the covers to my shoulders. Since the day had started off on such a sour note, I had to rectify it. I browsed through my phone's address book and searched. There had to be someone who was single and friendly enough to be my date.

"Emily Bursen," I mumbled to myself. "Nope, don't talk to her anymore." I scrolled down. "Sara Desler? No wait, she moved."

Christine Fencer. Mina Gordon. Adrienne Turner. All taken and all happy.

The despair in my stomach sank deeper as my phonebook hit the final letters of the alphabet. The rest of the names belonged to guys, except for one.

Pam Wicker.

Would it be that weird if I asked my best friend to prom?

My mind wrapped around the idea multiple times and the conclusion was always the same: we can attend the dance as friends. It doesn't have to mean anything.

At that moment a wave of anxiety slammed against my heart.

No, Pam was just a friend, nothing more. There was no reason to feel nervous about asking her. Was I hoping this opportunity would be the needed push to initiate a relationship with her? I laughed to myself; the idea was absolutely ludicrous.

Swept with boredom, I gazed around my room looking hopelessly for something to do. After a moment, I gave out a defeating sigh and settled on going for a drive. I ripped off my sweats and pulled on a pair of jeans and a sweater that was flung over the bedside lamp.

I climbed into my car and left in a rush. I drove down a major street looking for anything that even slightly caught my interest. Coffee shops, fast food joints, the local movie theater, some bookstores, but nothing was able to hold my gaze for more than few seconds. At that moment I felt a vibration in my pocket. My fingers dug in and retrieved my phone, finding a text message from Finn.

I pulled the car over and called him.

"Hello?" His voice sounded like he just woke up.

"What are you doing?"

"Nothing, what are you doing?" He yawned.

I didn't reply immediately. I spent a second wondering whether I should tell him about my plan to ask Pam to prom. I reached the conclusion that I should. That way I could find out whom he planned on asking.

"Can I come over?" I asked hastily.

"Yeah, sure."

We said goodbye after that and I zoomed off to Finn's house. He didn't live too far away so I arrived at his door in a matter of minutes.

"How's it going?" Finn asked as I stepped in.

I shrugged and followed him to his room.

"So what do you think?" He pointed towards a poster leaning against the wall.

If he hadn't brought it to my attention, I wouldn't have noticed the giant handmade billboard. I turned the poster around. Written in big black words were the phrase, "Will you go to prom with me?" Around the poster were elaborate designs and images that complemented the intended message.

My eyes slid away from the board and onto Finn. Before my mouth formed the first joke, he had already scoffed back. I let the witty remarks collapse and steered my words towards the topic at hand.

"So, who are you planning on asking?"

He stared back at me for a moment before replying casually, "Jackie Cobb."

I ran her name over in my head until a mental connection was made with Amber Stone. I didn't know what to say. The fact that Finn wanted to take Jackie, a cheerleader known for her bossy attitude, couldn't register with me. When I couldn't find any words to say, Finn changed the subject to me.

"And you, Blake?" He grinned at me. "Who do you plan on asking?"

"I was thinking...you know, Pam," I muttered.

"Ah, I see."

My heartbeat quickened and a million fears broke loose in my head. "What's wrong with me asking her?" I barked. "Is there any problem with taking a friend to a dance?"

Finn's expression flickered from drowsy to an amused state in an instant. His grin grew wider as if I had somehow become a sideshow freak. I quickly looked away and focused my stare on his hamper instead.

"Nothing wrong about that my friend," he said finally. "But I should warn you, Adam was planning on asking her too."

"Adam Crockford?" My head snapped back towards Finn.

"Uh, yeah."

"Football quarterback, Adam Crockford?"

"Uh, yeah."

Another complication in my life. If we both asked, whom would she choose? I exhaled heavily as my chances of finding a date suddenly diminished again. My expression must've been easy to read since Finn tried to comfort me.

"But you're her friend, I'm sure you stand on equal ground. I mean...sure, Adam is a school heartthrob or whatever, but knowing Pam, I'm sure she'll want to go with someone she's comfortable with."

Those words were enough to light a small fire of hope inside me. I had to remind myself to thank Finn later for his sincere words.

"When does he plan on asking her?" My voice came out surprisingly calm and even.

"I think tomorrow."

"Then I should ask her today."

Finn looked at me up and down. "Have you prepared anything?"

"No..." I felt defeated.

He gave out a sigh before lifting himself off the bed. He walked over to the sign he made, picked it up, and handed it to me.

"Use this. It's too tacky for me anyways." Finn laughed.

Instead of saying thank-you, I captured Finn in a tight hug. "I owe you one, big time!"

"So what are you waiting for? Let's go."

We hurried out the door and slid into my car. Butterflies fluttered in my stomach again and my feelings of anxiety reached a dangerous high. By the time we reached Pam's house, my breathing had grown irregular and my body felt dehydrated, probably due to the intensive sweating. Finn had to practically drag me out the car and for that split second I wished Pam had already found a date. I flickered my eyes in every direction as I followed the path leading up to her house, looking for any kind of distraction.

But there were none—no neighbors taking a stroll, no dogs barking, as if everything and everyone wanted to pay witness. We came to a sudden halt at the front of the yard and I felt very unfamiliar with the area, as if this was my first time at Pam's house.

"What are you waiting for?" Finn spat at me.

"Hold on, I'm mentally preparing," I snapped back.

I drew in a couple deep breaths, bent down and swiped a couple pebbles. I clutched the sign with one hand and drew the other back as if I was throwing a baseball. I tossed the pebbles one by one at Pam's window. Her bedroom was on the second floor and luckily faced the yard. There were a couple of clinks as the pebbles bounced off. Once again, my heart raced uncontrollably. It took exactly twelve seconds before the window drew open, revealing a drowsy Pam, her appearance in complete disarray.

"Okay, good luck, man." Finn whispered to me and then ran to my car and closed the door shut.

My brain felt scattered and I couldn't figure out what to do next. I felt my eyebrows wrinkling in confusion as my fingers tingled with excitement or fear, one of the two I couldn't be sure. I looked up at her as she wiped the sleep from her eyes. I glanced down and found the board clutched between my hands. Instinctively, I shoved the sign in the air and held it up. My eyes flickered towards Pam and captured her gaze. Her lips cracked into a smile and a small giggle escaped.

She nodded once and covered her face, probably embarrassed. She waved goodbye and flew from the window. I couldn't contain my grin as I skipped back to my car. The bounce in my step and the joy in my movement endured long after Finn and I left. For the rest of the day, we discussed plans for prom, mostly concerning tux and limo rentals. But I didn't mind being festive; this was an occasion I wanted to remember.

"Okay, so we still have to get our tuxes and rent a limo." Finn sighed. "Do we need to do anything else?"

"Limo is kind of expensive if it's just split between us," I noted.

"Just us two?"

"Well, we're not going to make the girls pay."

He nodded glumly. "Right."

"We can always share with some other people..."

"But who?" Finn looked thoughtful for a moment. "What about Jack and Bill Gavin?"

"The twins? Are they even going?" I said.

"Yeah, I talked to them about it in homeroom," Finn replied, smiling.

"Well, anyone is fine." I glanced at the clock and realized that dusk had fallen. "I should probably get going. Catch you later, bro."

Finn walked me out and I ventured into the night. My eyes squinted due to the brisk New York air, but I paid it no mind. The weather couldn't bring my mood down—there were more important things that captivated my attention. The only downside to a swamped head was the lack of awareness to everything else.

• • •

It seemed like only a minute had passed that I found myself blinking in the afternoon sky outside Pam's house. My tux was on and the limo was waiting behind me. I didn't have to think about what to do next, my body was able to move without my head telling it to. My legs moved mechanically to the door and I knocked three times.

Pam's dad answered the door. I wasn't surprised, but at the same time, my tongue doubled in size and my words came out scrambled. "Err, good day sir...um, I'm here to pick up... Uh, err, Pam, your daughter, to uh, prom. Yeah."

"Relax Blake, she's right there." He nodded towards the foot of the stairs where a goddess was gracefully coming down. I couldn't help but stare, and at that moment I didn't care if her dad caught me gawking—this was a sight to behold.

The mere sight of Pam stopped my breath. It didn't take long to figure out why. I never noticed her delicate frame before. I looked at Pam with inappropriate eyes, gazing at how her midnight blue dress hugged tightly around her slender shoulders, and her hair curling down where it rested perfectly on the edge of her neck. Everything about her was just amazing—no, breathtaking.

"How do I look?" She twirled in a circle when she reached me.

The corners of my lips tugged up and I couldn't resist the building smile. "Beautiful."

"You don't have to lie, Blake."

"I wish I was."

Her eyes widened for a second before a small laugh escaped her full lips. It seemed like my answer was what she was hoping for.

"Ready?" I extended an arm towards her.

Pam nodded and grasped my arm. I bid her dad good-bye before helping her into the limo.

We sat next to Finn and his date, Jackie Cobb. She shot me a few dirty glances throughout the trip, but I guess I had it coming—she was on the same squad as Amber Stone after all, and a close friend of Cory's. Once everyone was accounted for, the limo's wheels screeched off to the docks to board *The Azure*, the stage for our at-sea prom.

When we arrived, Jack, Bill, and their dates exited first. Pam stood up before I did and I knew the orderly conduct of a gentleman. I shoved her down and flew from the limo. She came out looking bewildered, but when I offered my hand, she smiled, understanding, and took it.

We spent most of the time dancing under the night sky. At certain points, we took a short break and grabbed a drink, but before I could inhale and exhale in the same breath, I was on the dance floor again. The clock chimed midnight and although we were dancing for the past three hours I wasn't able to fully savor the night. I was disappointed prom was ending so soon, but at the very least, I had a great time with my date.

"I love this song!" Pam gasped.

It was a slow song. The DJ had saved the best for last. I guess having the excuse to put both arms around Pam wasn't the worst way to end the night.

I decided to initiate it first.

My hands shook as I placed them on her waist. She flashed me a cute smile before putting hers around my neck. She gazed into my eyes from underneath her lashes and the bliss I felt at that moment was incomparable.

The song fit well with the night, ending sooner than I expected it to. A few seconds passed before I realized I was still holding her after the song's last note. I reluctantly ripped my hands away from Pam and cursed under my breath.

"Well, that was fun." I laughed nervously.

She tousled my hair. "Come on, let's go find Finn and get out of here."

I followed as she pushed through the hordes of bodies. I kept my gaze fixated on her, just her. I didn't know what I was feeling, but what I did know is that I didn't want to escape this sudden high.

"Blake!" someone called behind us. "Pam!"

My head whipped around and I saw Finn and Jackie bouncing towards us. Pam was still pushing forward so, I curled my hand around hers and dragged her in the opposite direction.

To my surprise, she didn't pull away. We reached our friend and only when he shot us a weird look did I force my hand back into my pocket.

"Where were you the whole night?" Pam asked Finn.

"The question is, where were you and Blake the whole night?" he stroked his chin.

Pam's face blushed a bright pink, which caught me completely off guard. Her eyes trailed the invisible line to mine and my words came out stumbling, "Umm... we were, you know," I said.

Finn laughed and gave me a pat on the back. "I'm glad you two had fun...right?" His tone came out nosy. Not wanting to answer any more questions about our evening, I did what any person would do in an awkward situation—point out the black sheep.

Jackie looked uncomfortable standing behind Finn so I pushed the spotlight onto her.

"How about you, Jackie?" I tried pathetically to sound friendly. "Did you have a good time with my boy here?"

She didn't respond immediately. First, she glowered at me and then turned away.

"It was fine. I'm just disappointed you guys didn't run into Cory and Amber tonight," she sneered at me.

"I think Cory is the one who should be avoiding him," Finn joked lightly.

Pam and Jackie rolled their eyes at his unnecessary remark.

"So, um...you guys want to get out of here?" I suggested.

They complied naturally and we made off the cruise ship where Jack and Bill and their dates were waiting with the limo.

"Took you guys long enough!" Bill cried. "We were about to leave without you!"

Finn apologized for all of us before helping Jackie step into the car. I did the same for Pam but not before flushing a little.

As I lay in bed thinking about graduation and my upcoming year at Brown, I found my thoughts plagued with the distress of not seeing Pam every day. If there was one regret during prom, it was not kissing her. I draped the blanket over my head and told myself not to think about it, but the more times I told myself, the more I did. I forced my eyes shut and clenched my jaw, determined to believe that whatever feelings I had for Pam were temporary and would disappear by tomorrow. It wasn't until the crack of dawn that my relentless teeth grinding stopped. Exhaustion crept over my thoughts and tossed me out of reality.

• • •

After prom, life danced by on the hands of time and I found myself being fitted into a graduation gown. It seems like the puzzle pieces of my life were coming together quite nicely, except for one piece, the one that held onto my heartstrings. My attraction towards Pam took a sudden spike recently that I couldn't look at her without getting jittery. Luckily, I did what came naturally, I smothered and hid my feelings but the aching grew worse with every passing day.

"The sleeves are a little long," my mom noted, breaking the daydream I was in. "And what about the cap, is it too tight for your head, Blake?

I let my arms fall to my sides. "Everything is perfectly fine, Mom. I don't know why you're so worried about how I look. I mean, I'm the one graduating, not you." I gave her a little smirk.

Her eyes blazed in retaliation.

"I'm just kidding! Geez, relax, Mom!" I threw my hands in front of me defensively.

She kissed me on the cheek. "I just want you to look handsome for the big day tomorrow."

"Uh, thanks I guess," I grumbled.

Tomorrow was graduation, which meant my days as a stupid teenager were nearing an end. I felt extraordinary inside, eager for the next step in my life.

"Remember that your dad and I won't be home in the morning to wake you up. We need to stop by the office, so it's your responsibility to get there on time," my mom nagged.

I bellowed something incoherent, lumbered back to my room and fell on my bed. I managed to get ten minutes of rest before my phone vibrated. It was Pam asking what I was doing. We conversed for a bit and agreed to meet for a cup of coffee. I knew I shouldn't feel ecstatic that Finn couldn't make it, but I felt that way nonetheless.

The little shop was small yet classy. Across the window in shiny gold letters read *Café Artiste*. I laughed to myself wondering where in the world Pam heard of a place like this.

A small bell over the door tinkled as I stepped inside. I scanned the menu and took my time walking to the cashier. With helpful suggestions from the worker, I settled on a cappuccino and a plate of almond cookies, which were Pam's favorite kind of cookies. I found a tiny table in the back fit for two and sat there. My stomach experienced queasiness and my head suffered through conflicting thoughts: Does this count as a date, or is this just a friend outing?

"Good afternoon Blake," said a soft voice. I looked up slowly. Pam stood beside me. I struggled to find words but my mouth felt small, as if my tongue had swelled three times the normal size and was now choking me.

"Hey, Pam," was all I could manage to say.

"Ooh, almond cookies. Good choice." She winked as she pulled out a chair and sat across from me.

"They're for you," I replied awkwardly.

Her eyes lit up and I had to resist buying all of the almond cookies available. After the first few moments of conversation, my tongue had rescinded to normal and talking became comfortable. We joked about graduation and plans for summer, and discussed grimly about the distance between our schools. We chatted long after the almond cookies disappeared and our coffee drinks were empty. But even then I felt like time was going by too fast. It felt unnatural to part with her after that, I wanted nothing more but to cling to her side like two opposite ends of a magnet.

"I'll see you tomorrow at graduation. Have a good night Blake, and thanks again for hanging out with me!" Pam waved goodbye as she climbed into her car.

"Anytime," I said quietly before marching back to mine. My head fell back on the headrest as I wondered whether or not Pam should be made aware of these feelings.

I shook my head in defiance, reminding myself that she didn't see me that way. To my relief, that seemed to work and I was able to get home emotionally unscathed.

The next morning I woke with a yawn and rubbed my eyes raw. Drowsiness clung to me like a baby probably because I spent most of the night feeling excited for today. After another yawn and a quick glance at the clock, my heart skipped a beat.

Graduation had already started. I was already half an hour late. It would be stupid to show up to the ceremony now. Was it that important to me, to graduate with the rest of my class? The answer to that question was yes. I wanted to leave high school beaming with satisfaction and plus my mom will kill me if I wasn't there.

I drew in a sharp breath and set Time Waver to an hour previous. I closed my eyes and jabbed the red button. The time-traveling breeze didn't bother me any more and it almost felt relaxing. My eyes flickered open and I was back in bed. I glanced at the clock and sure enough, I was exactly on schedule. I grabbed my gown and cap before bouncing out the door. At school, the parking lot was nearly full. I locked my car and walked quickly to the gym where the rest of my classmates would be.

"There you are!" Finn pushed people aside to get to me. "I've been looking everywhere for you."

"Blake!" Pam squealed, slapping the side of my arm. "I thought you were going to be late."

I apologized to them, and then we clambered up to form a line. One by one we were passed a card where we were to write our name. It wasn't long before the sound of the school band thumped its way into our ears. I glanced at Pam first and then Finn, both were smiling eagerly. My lips curled up as well. I didn't bother fighting it. It was time to graduate.

"Everyone here? Well, it doesn't matter, it's time to start now anyways," one of the teachers said. "March quickly and file into the seats. Don't linger but don't walk too fast either. Okay, here we go."

We walked as a unit from the gym and onto the smooth, damp grass. The crowd's cheers were deafening. The body count on the bleachers was enough to cast most of the football field in its shadow. The drone of hundreds of voices continued even after we finished sitting down. Only when our principal touched the microphone did the thundering stop.

"Hello all! We are all gathered here today to join in celebration. Sitting here before me are three hundred of the finest young men and women to ever grace this school. It brings me great joy to share this experience with you all. I know for a fact that this will be a time to remember. Proud parents, aunts, uncles, cousins, all family, I present to you this year's class!"

My eyes, however, weren't fixated on our principal. Instead, I found it lingering on Pam. I studied her face, memorizing how her nose crinkled a bit before tears formed and how her eyes twinkled in the right lighting.

"Now, one row at a time. Come up here and receive your diploma."

My eyes locked with Pam's for a split second. I flickered them away immediately. I swallowed, wondering whether or not she caught me staring. I decided to play it cool and follow what everyone else was doing. I clapped enthusiastically for my classmates when they went up for their turn in the spotlight. Pretty soon my row was called. We stood up in unison and marched towards the front. We stopped a few feet shy and gave our name cards to the teacher.

"Terry Aber!" the principal shouted.

A small boy with light blond hair stumbled on the stairs and almost fell over. But he managed to reach the principal and get his diploma. After that came Dorothy Coney, Billiam Webb, James Lewis, and Aimee Browning.

"Finn Evans!" the principal cried.

A loud cheer erupted as Finn walked smugly to get his diploma. He turned around to give me a thumbs-up before a teacher forcefully ushered him off the stage.

"Pam Wicker!"

The whole football field burst into applause, louder than what Finn received. I drew back in surprise at how much affection she'd gained. Her face glowed bright pink as she walked carefully up the steps in her heels. It was my turn next and I inhaled a deep breath.

"Blake Dawson!"

I smiled weakly as everyone clapped for me. It was weird being the center of attention. I never understood how Finn was able to take it so gracefully. I stepped forward and shook the principal's hand. He winked and mouthed a quick "good job". I accepted the diploma and proceeded off the stage. My eyes did a quick scan of the crowd and found my parents in the dead center. My dad was smiling and my mom was crying and waving. I flashed them a bright smile and waved back before returning to my seat.

My grin didn't disappear until graduation ended. Even then, my happiness levels were at an all-time high. I was finally done with high school and felt satisfied with my time there. I can close that part of my life and move on to the next. The idea of attending an ivy-league school didn't stress me out that much, I still had Time Waver and planned on using it whenever necessary. Everyone always says how life is full of surprises, but how great is it that I can predict when those surprises would occur and how to utilize them to realize my full potential?

6
Summer Sun

IT WASN'T HARD to buy into the idea that summer was a blissful time for any student, no matter the age. Most kids use the first half of break to spend time with their families, friends, and hobbies. The second half either comes with a feeling of dread for the new school year or an explosion of excitement. I fell into a category between the two. I was ignoring the dread and excitement, just focusing on the now.

Pam, Finn and I planned on spending the first half of our summer together. The second half was reserved for visiting our schools and getting situated in their environment. The first few days we bummed around at each other's houses, doing everything from movie marathons to board game nights. This night we were playing monopoly at my house.

"Trade me for Park Place!" Finn pressed. "Come on I'll give you two yellows!"

I looked from him to Pam to my monopoly properties. "Let me think for a second…"

"Don't do it, Blake! He already has Boardwalk. Do you want to lose?" Pam's eyebrows furrowed.

Finn shot her a glance. "Hey, you're not a part of this! This is our deal, not yours. So mind your own business! Just sit there and look pretty for us." He grinned triumphantly.

She hissed at him before turning back to me. "Please don't."

"Sorry Finn, but I can't let the danger of Park Place and Boardwalk fall on us," I said stiffly and then gave Pam a little wink.

She giggled mockingly at Finn and in retaliation, he cursed at us. The truth was that the game was dragging, but I felt an irrational need to comply with whatever Pam wanted me to do. It was sad and kind of pathetic, but that was the least of my worries. Once the college train hit us, our destinations would be different. And there I would throw away my unrequited feelings for Pam and move on with my life. But for now, just for now, I wanted to please myself just a bit longer.

"Your turn, Blake!" Pam chirped.

She handed me the dice and I felt a surge of electricity when our fingers touched. I rolled and moved accordingly, and with my luck, I landed on Pam's hotels. It was a bittersweet feeling since I wanted to win, but it was enough satisfaction to watch Pam's face light up.

"I don't think I have enough money." I frowned as I handed her what I had.

"It's okay, I can take an IOU."

I shook my head. "Nope, I lost fair and square. You can have my properties as the rest of the compensation."

"Are you sure? Because really, it's fine."

"I'm sure." I handed her all my properties and threw my token back inside the box.

"Hey, that's not fair!" Finn objected. "You guys are cheating!"

"How?" Pam shot back.

"You can't give each other properties!"

"House rules."

I laughed.

"Whatever. I'll still beat you either way!" Finn snarled.

I leaned my head back and watched the game progress. Finn was able to hold out for a while, but Pam's empire had grown too big. He landed on her spaces like a rabbit bouncing around in a landmine field.

"I win, I win, I win!" Pam went around gloating.

"You got lucky," Finn grumbled. He put his fist into the air and shook it viciously.

Pam rolled her eyes before collapsing on the couch. I looked over at her, staring with blank eyes. It took a while for her to notice me, but I didn't hesitate to flicker my glance away.

"So what do you guys want to do tomorrow?" Pam yawned.

Everyone looked thoughtful for a moment before Finn replied, "Well, me and Blake only have a week left before we have to go to Brown for orientation. When are you flying to LA again?"

"In two weeks!"

I attempted to mend my facial expression so that it appeared like I was excited for her, but underneath the façade, I wasn't too pleased. Luckily, by the time I settled into a chair, the conversation moved onto different subjects.

"So, will you guys be dorming together?" Pam asked.

Finn replied for us, "Yeah, already sent in the paperwork and stuff."

"Lucky...I'm scared that my roommate might not like me."

"What's not to like?" I said smoothly, while Finn on the other hand, laughed heartily.

"Thank you Blake." She giggled, her eyes twinkling.

I would've flushed at her words, but suddenly, the room began to spin and my eyes went hazy. At the same time, a sharp pain shot down my spine. My back went rigid as stone and I began to breathe heavily.

"Is something wrong?" Finn asked.

"N-no, I-I'm fine."

The pain didn't last very long. It was a sudden spurt, disappearing as fast as it began. What felt worse was the sense of panic that attacked my thoughts. How could my body be breaking down so easily?

"Let's meet up tomorrow," I gasped.

Both Finn and Pam shot me a worried look.

"Don't worry, I'm fine! I'm just tired from that epic game." I faked a yawn and rubbed my eyes.

They exchanged glances but in the end, they gathered their things and left. I watched through the window for a while, waiting for both cars to pull out before walking to my room and getting into bed. I rolled over and threw the blanket over my head. My body felt numb and exhausted even though the sudden pain trauma had only lasted a few seconds. But it was okay, since I needed the rest. I should try to recover as much as I could before putting Time Waver to use at Brown.

The rest of the week didn't crawl by like I expected. But when Finn and I were on the way to Brown for orientation, I felt ecstatic. We took his car since we decided that my car probably couldn't make the trip. The good thing about feeling this excited was that it pushed any other thoughts out of my head. I didn't have time to think about Pam or my wasting health, I only had one thought: how to succeed at Brown.

"Man, how far is this place? I'm so tired," Finn complained.

"Dude, you just started driving," I snorted.

I rested my head on the seat, exhaling happily that I had finished my shift of driving this morning. Finn was too sleepy to get behind the wheel so I went first. The trip was roughly four hours, so we split into two driving sessions. Finn was only thirty minutes in and he was already yawning like an oversized sloth. But in the end he managed to pull himself together to finish the trip without much complaint.

We arrived to a banner stretching across two trees: Welcome New Brown Bears!

"Look over there!" Finn pointed.

"Where?"

"Where all the other jokers are lining up."

"We should probably head there then." I slapped him on the back.

The chatter in the air was energizing and intimidating at the same time. Although the kids in line babbled to one another, their gazes intently stared ahead. Finn and I waited in the back, trying to figure out the purpose of this line. We didn't have to wait long since at that moment two staff members ushered everyone into an auditorium. After the initial introduction, we had a couple hours to familiarize with the campus before getting the tour of our dorms. Finn and I roamed around, peeking our heads in every crack and nook of the place. College campuses seemed enormous compared to a high school, but luckily, people were friendly and had no problems with pointing us in the right direction. During the dorm tour, for some reason, I found myself out of breath multiple times, while Finn seemed fine. I wondered why walking around and exploring the campus had me heaving for air. And then a single thought struck me like a bolt of lightning.

Was it another side effect to Time Waver?

That was a possibility no matter how hard I tried to deny it.

"Come on Blake, keep up!" Finn said. "Geez how out of shape are you?"

I didn't reply.

We spent the remainder of the trip exploring our future living quarters. The rooms were decent enough, small but cozy. It had one bathroom and a desk right next to each bed, which of course, is where I should be spending most of my time, hunched over the table lamp. Finn meanwhile, probably wouldn't need to buy a single textbook.

The drive back didn't take nearly as long as the drive there. Since it was nighttime, fewer cars were on the road. We managed to reach home a little earlier than expected. I decided to call Pam, not because I wanted to tell her all about Brown, it was simply because I missed her.

Pam was at *Café Artiste* sitting by herself, sipping coffee and turning the pages of a worn-out magazine. I walked up behind her and grasped her by the shoulders, shaking her lightly. Her head whipped around and our eyes locked for a second. I noticed her lips were on the verge of breaking into a smile before the sound of a chair squeaking broke the moment. Finn was sitting with a sheepish grin smacked across his face.

"Was I interrupting something?" he asked, still grinning broadly.

"No of course not!" Pam said, a little too fast for my liking.

I pulled out a chair too and sat, my body leaning closer to hers than Finn's. We sat in silence for a moment, none of us wanting to strike up a conversation yet, I guessed.

Pam squashed the silent bug. "How was Brown? Meet any cute girls?"

Finn and I exchanged glances. "Nope, we had no time to go scouting."

"Oh really now?"

"Really! They kept us busy with all the walking and talking," I continued, but then paused to steal a sip of Pam's coffee. "The dorms are pretty nice though, clean and tidy."

Finn rolled his eyes. "Yeah, that's what we care about... our living space."

I changed the subject. "What about you? What did you do all day?"

Pam looked at me as if the answer was obvious. I gave her an empty look.

"Pretty much this. Sitting around and waiting for you guys to come home."

"Well, we're probably going to do the same when you leave for orientation." I laughed.

"At least you guys have each other for company! I will be alone when I go to orientation too!"

"Think about it this way, if you're alone, more guys will probably hit on you." Finn cracked a joke before laughing.

"I wouldn't mind if cute boys come talk to me," Pam added.

I laughed along although it probably came out fake. Even if it was a joke, I didn't care much for it. Pam wasn't my girlfriend or anything and I really had no foundation to carry any jealousy but that was something I couldn't help. Adoration makes the most irrational choices and decisions become the most logical ones.

It was quiet for a while until Pam suddenly yelped. Finn and I looked at her with surprised expressions. "What is it?" I asked, a little worried.

"I need to give you two your gift!" she said excitedly. "Well, it's for both of you to share." Pam didn't speak another word as she threw herself out of her seat and ran towards her car. I exchanged glances with Finn before settling into my chair, waiting for Pam to return.

She tossed a bag on the table. "Open it!" she hissed at us.

Finn had his arms crossed and motioned for me to check what it was. I sighed as I rose up and opened the paper bag. I pulled out two webcams.

"They're for us to communicate while we're at college!" She looked hopeful.

But her face shined disappointment when my expression and Finn's didn't display the same excitement. The truth was that I wasn't excited at all to see Pam over a webcam. I wanted to see and talk to her in real life. Conversing over the Internet just wouldn't cut it for me. But the gift was thoughtful and was better than nothing.

I put on a fake smile. "That's great really! Can't believe you're thinking so far ahead."

Finn nodded agreeing, but didn't comment on her gift. The rest of the night passed quickly. By the time I got home, I was exhausted. I passed out almost immediately and dreamt about something I was likely to forget in the morning.

• • •

It seemed like time was both my enemy and my friend. Although I had the power to travel back in it, there was no way to slow it down. How much time is one's life really? Just a blink compared to entities like the sun or the earth. My summer was easily comparable to that. With just another blink, it was over and I found myself reluctantly packing my belongings. My dad had agreed to drive me up there and help me settle in. But he didn't agree to help me pack. I carried the boxes one by one and stacked them in the trunk of his car. I asked what he planned on doing with my Trans-Am since I wouldn't need it up in Brown. He said modestly that he already had a couple buyers lined up to look at it. Apparently, my baby was going to help pay for my tuition. I had no qualms about this, and I merely nodded.

Throughout the trip, my dad talked—more like lectured—me on the dangers of college. I tried to pay attention but zoning out sounded like a more appealing thing to do. By the time the sun closed on the horizon, we were unloading the car of my possessions. My pop didn't seem like he was in a hurry so I didn't rush him home. We managed to stack all my boxes in one corner of the room. Finn hadn't arrived yet, so the law of dibs took effect. I chose the bed closest to the window and left Finn with the bed near the door.

I chuckled mischievously as I unpacked my bed sheets, blanket, and pillows and threw them on the bed. My dad kept busy with folding clothes into a dresser until someone knocked on the door. I walked to it and swung it open. In front of me was a lady around her early to mid-forties and sported an old-school haircut.

"Hello, my name is Ms. Terry. I'm the campus advisor for this block." She stuck out her hand and I weakly shook it. My dad let out a cough behind me, warning me without words that my manners had to be present.

"I'm Blake Dawson and this is my dad—"

"Richard Dawson, pleasure is ours." My dad shook her hand. "So, what can we do for you?"

She gave a little smile. "I'm here to make sure everything is going fine."

"Fine it is."

I looked from my dad to Ms. Terry to my dad again. They were engaged in what can only be described as an impromptu staring contest. Only when Finn and his dad arrived did the connection break.

"Hey Blake, what's up?" Finn said rather energetically. But his energy soon died once he saw I had already chosen the window bed. He threw me a fierce look as he unpacked his stuff on the reject bed. I glanced at my dad again and found him conversing with Ms. Terry and Finn's dad. I pushed whatever weird thoughts I had about my dad and the campus advisor out of my mind and went back to unpacking. Five minutes later, my dad informed us he and Finn's pop were going to get coffee.

I nodded with a clenched jaw. I didn't want to ask if he had invited Ms. Terry too...

No.

My dad was in love with my mom. He had to be.

I shook my head furiously once my dad left and drew in a couple of deep breaths. Finn was too busy with his own things to pay me any attention, which was good because I was in no mood to answer any questions.

It wasn't long before my mood brightened again. I was being paranoid. After a couple posters were hung up and looking good, our dorm was starting to feel like home.

"So what should we do now?" Finn asked, sitting on his bed.

I plugged my laptop into a free outlet. "I'm going to see if Pam is done settling in yet. We promised we would webcam tonight..." I checked my watch. It was barely eight. "She probably just got off her plane. Probably another two hours until she's ready," I noted glumly. But even so,

I set up the webcam anyway and made sure it was up and running for tonight.

I fell into the bed and stared at the ceiling. Finn was staying quiet as well so my mind drifted off again. But I couldn't keep the Zen state for long since a loud knock thrust me back into my dorm room. Finn and I exchanged glances, mind-battling to see who would get the door. I won with logic on my side. Finn's bed was closer to the door and Finn was on his bed, therefore, he was closer to the door and should get it.

It turned out to be our parents, coming to say goodbye and wishing us luck in school. We were glad they weren't our moms; otherwise it would've been a lot more emotional. My dad's goodbye consisted of a couple grunts, murmurs, and an awkward hug.

"I'm going to shower," I said when our fathers left.

He nodded like it was a reflex as he sat there browsing the web. It was weird at first for me to grab clothes and bring them into the shower, but that was something I had to adjust to. The water turned warm quickly and I allowed my body to soak up the heat. It felt refreshing, good enough where I closed my eyes and allowed my mind to sink into thoughts. I contemplated matters on my unrequited love for Pam, the start of semester, and my life span, which by far seemed the most trivial compared to the first two thoughts. I didn't know how long I let the water run for but the sudden knocking had alerted me I had been in here for a while. I turned off the nozzle and called to see what Finn wanted.

"It's Pam!" He shouted back. "She told us to get online!"

I quickly dried myself and threw on clothes. I stopped for a brief moment to fix my hair in an attempt to look at least half-decent. Once I couldn't look at my reflection any further without risking turning into an egomaniac, I exited the bathroom and found Finn at my computer. I sat next to him and held my breath. Suddenly, as if it was a new day starting, Pam appeared on the screen. Her face was glowing and her teeth shining.

"Hey guys!" she said. "I just finished settling in and meeting my roommate! What are you guys doing?"

"Nothing," we said at the same time.

"Where's your roommate now?" Finn asked.

"In the bathroom."

"She pretty?"

Pam rolled her eyes. "I'm not hooking you up with anyone, Finn."

He scowled at her and she giggled in response. The sound of her chirping laugh somehow warmed my insides. It was probably weird to think about, but it felt good to hear it. We chatted for a while before she had to sign off. Pam and her roommate planned on getting a late-night bonding dinner. Once she disappeared from my screen I felt an aching in my chest. I was missing her already and it had only been a day. I wondered what would be harder on me—the courses at Brown or the lack of seeing Pam.

It was most likely the latter.

7
Hard Work

NO DOUBT IN my mind, the most boring class I had was Economics. Professor Burt was an old man with a deep monotone voice. He held the ability to eliminate caffeine from one's body and place them under his drowsiness spell.

Calculus, taught by Professor Stein, wasn't too shabby. She was a tiny woman who had to jump a few times to pull down the projector. At the start of the class she always introduced herself, no one knew why but humored her regardless.

English was the same as any other English class I've taken. Professor Ordell wasn't the strictest teacher around, but he sure knew how to overload the coursework. At the start of our first class he gave us a timed essay and then a prompt for homework, all on the same day.

"Writing is like a sword," he said. "If you don't use it, it'll wither and rust. But if you use it often, it stays sharp and ready."

It wasn't the best motivation speech but it did establish some poetic justice. The aspiring writers in his class especially, couldn't wait to get started and show him their talents with a pen.

The class I most looked forward to was at the end of my day, Business Administration. It would be a blessing if I learned all the necessary skills to run a company efficiently. The teacher, Professor Mai was a little ways from being the ideal instructor. He blurted out wise-ass jokes and his lesson plan was scattered and inconsistent with the syllabus he handed out.

I was relieved when I found out I wasn't the only person feeling overwhelmed. It's only been two weeks and more than half the kids in our freshman class could be diagnosed with anxiety issues. I felt a little guilty that I possessed the power to turn the tables in my favor, but it disappeared quickly. I remembered that here, and unlike the adolescent years of high school, that no one cared if I succeeded, they only cared about themselves and their own success.

The rest of the week zoomed by at a grinding pace. I was so overloaded with research papers and statistical analysis work that Friday brought a much-needed break. Finn and I headed to the dining hall to discuss our classes. We'd barely spoken a word this week since our time schedules were so different. When I didn't have class, he did and when he was fast asleep, I was alert and awake.

"So you feeling pressured yet?" I asked Finn before grabbing a bagel off the tray.

"A little. History is quite a drag and I don't really care for it. The teacher for my Sociology class is pretty smoking though. So that's a plus."

"Sure that won't distract you?"

We found a table by the window and sat.

"I think I'll be fine in my classes. I'm worried about you," Finn said.

"What do you mean?"

"This place isn't easy like Cristo Rey, as you already know."

I took a bite and chewed slowly, calculating how I should phrase my unshakable confidence.

"I think I can handle it. I was barely trying back in high school."

He laughed. "Yeah, I remember you suddenly switched it up. Getting all A's right at the very end."

"I had to start trying sometime, you know." I shrugged, taking another bite.

Silence fell on our table as we munched on our food. Finn inhaled his bowl of porridge, while I took my time nibbling at the bagel. I stretched my hands in the air after breakfast and asked Finn what his plans were for the day. He didn't have the faintest idea. My gaze flickered around the room and I found people segregated into groups, most of them shaking with laughter.

"Well, it's Friday," I said.

He ignored my remark.

"Dude, it's Friday," I repeated.

"What about today?" Finn said with raised eyebrows.

My lips curled up into a half-smile.

"Isn't the homecoming rally today?" I sneered gleefully.

"Yeah, but I think it's too late to buy any tickets."

I rolled my eyes. "I don't think we need tickets for the after parties, bro."

"Oh true! We should socialize with our peers. And by peers, I mean the girls!" he said as his eyes blazed with joy.

I fed off his energy and tried to make it my own. The truth was that I just wanted to get my mind off of Pam.

Finn stood up, cleared his plate, and stretched around. "Should we start checking around?"

"For the parties?"

"Yeah."

"You can start first," I said quietly. "I'm going to finish my breakfast."

"Alright, I guess. You sure are taking your time with that bagel." His lips twitched in amusement.

He strutted to a nearby table and initiated a conversation. After a moment, laughter chimed through the air and the next I caught Finn's eye. He gave me a sudden wink and continued the chitchat.

I returned to my bagel and gave it unnecessary attention. I took small bites. My stomach felt queasy and unsettled. Was it because of the bagel or had my lack of nutrition this past week caught up to me? I sighed deeply and threw the rest of the bagel into my mouth. I clenched my jaw and forced my teeth to shred the food.

There was movement in the chair next to mine and I found Finn sitting beside me with a creepy grin on his face. "The deed is done," he said triumphantly.

I took a second to swallow my food. "You found an open party we can go to?"

"Man, who do you think you're talking to...of course I found one!"

I opened my mouth to take a shot at his arrogance but decided against it. Finn did deserve some praise after all.

Afterwards, we returned to our dorm room. I climbed into bed and pulled the blanket tight around my shoulders. I wasn't sleepy but I closed my eyes anyways. I heard the bathroom door close shut as I shifted my body around until I felt comfortable.

For some reason my mind was racing but only had one thought.

How was Pam doing?

That thought circled inside my head, doing endless laps without any end in sight. It continued like that for the rest of the day. I didn't know her schedule or how busy she was. I wanted to call her every single night, but at the same time, I shouldn't be a nuisance when she wanted to study or hang with her dorm mates.

"Is there something wrong?" Finn asked me, when he emerged out of the shower. "You've been quiet all day, bro."

"Wh-what? N-no I'm fine." I stuttered, surprised I was being so obvious.

"Whatever you say, man. But you better be in a better mood when we hit up that party."

I nodded and continued to sulk for the rest of the day in miserable silence.

Ten minutes before midnight, we left the dorm and made our way across the school grounds. The party was at a frat house on the edge of campus. The place wasn't hard to find since the music was thumping. We walked inside and found a bunch of people in the mood to dance.

Someone appeared around the corner and approached Finn and I. His eyes squinted for a second as he tried to recognize us. "Hang onnnnn..." he slurred. "Finn, is that youuuu?"

Finn gave him a hug and assured him he was right.

He led us deeper into the house, struggling to balance himself on his feet. Drinks ranging from beer to vodka lined the tables and it seemed as though the corners of each room had become people's bedrooms.

"Man, this party is kind of wild, huh?" Finn said without turning around.

"I think that's an understatement." I stayed focused and tried not to trip over anybody who was facedown on the floor.

We stopped by the kitchen and poured ourselves a drink. I hadn't planned on drinking but the atmosphere of the place rid me of that resolve. After the first couple of shots, my body loosened up and the alcohol kept pouring. Pretty soon I didn't have to pretend to enjoy the party. Our senses became diluted and our actions, blurred.

The next morning I woke up in my own bed. My eyes glanced over to Finn's bed and he was sound asleep, snoring like an animal. I propped my pillow and sifted through yesterday's events looking to find the part where we went home, but sighed in defeat instead. I got up slowly and stumbled to the bathroom and washed my face repeatedly. It seemed like my body was functioning properly.

No bruises or scratches. No repercussions from last night, I guessed. I exited the bathroom and saw Finn sitting up. He had one palm against his cheek and the other across his forehead.

I chuckled. "Rough night?"

His expression showed no doubt to my words. His eyes couldn't even meet mine without being unfocused. He gave a small grunt and nodded. Our first college party ended in a blackout. As Finn and I walked to the dining hall for a late breakfast, our empty stomachs groaned and rumbled with every heavy footstep.

"What time is it?" Finn asked.

I glanced down to give him the information he wanted, but a bolt of shock struck me. Time Waver wasn't on my wrist. My heart skipped a couple beats and my body went cold from fear.

Finn's head whipped around. "Is something wrong, Blake?"

"My watch is missing." My voice came out shaking.

Finn's eyebrows furrowed.

"That watch is important to me." My hands were trembling now and I couldn't seem to rip my eyes away from my naked wrist.

"Maybe you left it at the party?" Finn suggested.

"I don't remember taking it off."

"Bro, we don't remember anything from last night."

My frustration built and I let it escape my lips. "NO!" I snapped, "Someone stole it, I'm telling you."

"No harm in checking right?" He shrugged. "So, how about we get breakfast first and then go look for your watch?"

I turned away. "I'm not that hungry. I'll go look first."

I sprinted away, not wanting to waste any time. The story of my success was riding on my watch and I lost it. I thought about how careless I was to let something so great slip through my fingers. My mind went into search and rescue mode as I combed through my memories.

Mental images of last night sifted through as I ran towards the frat house. I tried to piece different parts of the party together, doing my best to make sense of things. Why the hell would I take off my watch? Or, a better question is why would someone steal a watch that isn't a major brand? None of it made sense, but it was pointless to worry about that now. In a matter of minutes, I came to a crashing stop in front of the house. Both doors were closed; the silence was oddly unsettling.

I hesitated at first but the pause in my steps left quickly. I knocked hard and loud against the thick wooden doors. I didn't have to wait long until someone drew the door open.

"Yeah?" the guy who opened the door said. "Can I help you?"

"I lost a watch here last night. I need to go look for it."

He was too drowsy to oppose me so he let me through. I walked quickly inside and checked around the main room before backtracking to the kitchen. I searched frantically, checking all the cabinets, under the table, and even the oven. I groaned and moved to the living room, looking in every crack and space in this house. As the seconds ticked by, my mood plummeted. Hope was draining from me as if a doctor stuck a needle inside my vein and drew away everything that was good and pure. I sat on the couch for a moment and buried my face in my palms.

"What's going on?" a voice said behind me. "Who are you?"

I jumped to my feet, half hoping the mystery person would join me in my endeavor.

"If you're here for the party, it ended last night." He smirked.

This guy was different from the boy who opened the door. That kid was small and scrawny, while this guy looked big and confident.

I sighed deeply. "I'm looking for something I lost last night."

"What is it?"

"My watch, when I woke up this morning it was gone."

"So you think we stole your watch?" he barked, turning defensive.

"No, I'm just saying I lost it and I'm here to look for it."

He scowled and dug into his pocket. He pulled out an object and dangled it in front of him. "Is this what you're looking for?"

A wave of relief washed over me, cleansing my body from frustration and anxiety. "Yeah! Where was it?" I ran up to him and he dropped it in my palm.

"Found it on the kitchen counter this morning." He hiked up the stairs. The next second a door slammed shut.

I felt like it wasn't right to linger so I left the house quickly. The outside breeze weaved through my hair and I took in a fresh breath. I strapped Time Waver back on my wrist and drew in another breath.

Everything was back to normal. I whistled as I took my time going back to Finn. I made a mental promise to myself not to let another crisis like that happen again. If anything, they would have to cut my arm off in order to take my watch. I laughed heartily as I pictured it.

• • •

The rest of the semester flew by. It was a bit ironic that after I adjusted to Brown's campus it was time to pack up and enjoy winter vacation at home. My feet were planted here and I didn't want to leave, but there was one driving force that overpowered my desire to stay. Pam was flying back soon and every nerve in my body ordered me to go see her. With all the schoolwork and social activities we didn't get a chance to converse much throughout semester, so a chance to see her was something I couldn't pass up.

"Why are you taking so long to pack?" Finn was lying on his bed, his eyes turned towards me.

"Why were you so hasty?" I threw a few outfits into a bag.

"Dude, we're only going to be gone a couple weeks. It's not like you're moving out of the dorm. Why are you bringing so much stuff?"

I paused and thought about it. Finn was right.

"Who knows," was all I managed to say.

He sat up. "What's with the gloom, bro? Aren't you glad to see your family?"

"Of course, I'm fine really."

The truth was that deep inside I was panicking. One on hand I wanted to see Pam, but on the other I felt like it would be a bad idea. I didn't know where it stemmed from, all I know was that this kind of panic was incomparable, worse than finals week. Then again, Time Waver allowed me to control the outcome of my scores, but with Pam, I was completely and overwhelmingly powerless. Such confliction destroyed my composure, so much that even Finn noticed the not-so-subtle change in me.

"Then why do you look so worried?" Finn tried again to break through my defenses.

I glared at him. "I'm just concerned about my final grades," I grimaced, hoping to shift his attention towards his own classes.

Finn's dad and mine picked us up the following morning in the same car. Thirty minutes into the car ride, all questions concerning school and life were asked and answered. I kept myself occupied thinking about what courses I should take the following semester. The car ride doesn't seem to last very long when your mind was wandering. It's an amazing to thing to be able to have your eyes looking at reality, but its sight on a dream.

Once home, I unpacked, putting everything neatly away. I shuffled into the kitchen and found my mom whipping up dinner.

"How's school, Blake?" That was my mom's opener.

I turned around and gave her a look. "I'm not in elementary school, Mom. I know how to stay on top of things." I snorted.

"Dinner is almost done. Just sit there and look pretty then."

One of my eyebrows shot up. "Already done."

It was a weird experience eating with my folks again. Although I've been doing it since childhood, one step away into college had really changed things. It didn't feel normal without having another hundred kids sitting nearby talking about nonsense. The dinner table was quiet, almost eerie. I didn't give it much thought since the steak had full control of me. After dinner, I washed up and rendezvoused with Finn at a nearby park. We sat on the swings as the bright streetlights shined above us.

I swung back and forth, gazing off into the distance, partly wishing that Pam might cancel. I swung higher, my feet no longer touching the ground. I kept my eyes on the rigorous task of scanning the area, but it didn't have to work for long since a dark figure was closing in from the distance. Although the person was blurred, it was easy to realize whom the curvy frame belonged to.

I skidded to a stop and jumped off the swing. I took a step forward, and then another. Pretty soon it became a flat-out jog to meet her. I stopped a few feet short and drew in a few quick breaths. The action helped regulate my heartbeat, which pounded like it would explode at any second. As I treaded slowly, her face lit up with a smile. That was enough to send my blood racing. It's been several months since I've last seen Pam, but her smile was still potent enough to have that effect on me.

"Hey Blake, how have you been?" she said.

I grinned wider as my footsteps fell into place with hers.

"I'm doing good, not too shabby, I must say."

I tried to keep from staring at her but that proved to be a difficult feat.

"How about Finn? Still the same person?"

I glanced from her to Finn and then back to her. "Um, he's still as smart as ever, if that counts."

She giggled but then yelped. Her body bumped into mine. I managed to catch her around the waist before she fell.

"Sorry, I didn't see that rock," she said sheepishly as her cheeks went a little pink. It was probably brighter than I had thought, but the overhead streetlights made it hard to tell.

We matched stride for stride back to Finn who was still sitting on the swings. He got up slowly, brushed himself off and gave Pam a hug. He let her have the middle swing and sat on one side of her and me on the other.

Pam spoke first, "So, tell me about the Ivy-league life." Her tone tried to come off as mocking, but beneath the pitch was a layer of envy. I met Finn's eyes and nudged for him to answer.

"It's not that hard. I was expecting more." He shrugged with an arrogant grin smacked on his face.

"Really now?" Pam asked, skeptically.

"Really."

She shot me a look and I shrugged as well.

"You guys are just nerds then. I'm having the hardest time at UCLA." She paused to exhale heavily before continuing, "The teachers aren't friendly at all, most of my classmates are pricks, and to top it off, the workload is borderline suicidal. I haven't had a complete meal in weeks, my sleep schedule is erratic, and I have a pile of laundry that's stinking up my dorm. I think if it wasn't for Bruce I would be pushing up daisies right now."

My mind drew blank as I tried to connect the name Bruce with a face. But the fact of the matter was that I didn't know anyone with that name.

I couldn't resist the urge to ask, "Bruce?"

At first she looked at me with a puzzled expression but then it shifted to surprise.

"Oh, I'm sorry, I forgot to tell you guys about Bruce." She laughed a little. "Bruce Spencer to be exact."

"Okay then, who's Bruce?" I pressed.

"Um, he's kind of my...boyfriend."

My heart stopped cold but my mind drew fire. I became disoriented as a billion different questions weaved around in my mind. I understood what Pam had said, but couldn't seem to comprehend it. I failed to grasp the idea of her being with another guy, so much that I burst out laughing uncontrollably.

"What's so funny, bro?" Finn asked, laughing a little too.

I glanced at Finn and shook my head, still laughing. My eyes fell on Pam next. Her face showed more concern than amusement. After my brief hysterical stint and assurance I was perfectly sane, the conversation moved to more heart-wrenching topics. Finn bombarded Pam with questions about Bruce. I tried to drown them out and zone off, but my ears still caught everything I didn't want to hear.

Pam and Bruce met in history class.

Pam and Bruce became study buddies.

Pam and Bruce went out for coffee one night where he asked her on a date.

Pam said yes.

The frustration I felt at that moment was unforgivable. I should be ecstatic for Pam, be happy she found a reason for happiness in a place where she had to start from scratch.

My eyes flickered to Pam. A small smile broke in between her lips.

She was happy and I had to move on.

I told myself over and over again.

I swung slowly on the swing, deeply regretting I hadn't confessed my feelings to Pam...and for returning home this winter break.

8
Recovery

I SPENT THE rest of winter vacation cooped up in my room. The only time I left was for basic human needs: hunger and hygiene. I feigned sickness, a typical excuse when you didn't want to see anyone, or in my case, a particular someone.

A half an hour past noon on Sunday, Finn and I headed back to Brown. Pam had flown out the day before. I fought the urge to text her goodbye. I scoffed at how spiteful I was being, but I couldn't care less. The sun shone bright, making the grass glisten and sparkle as it swayed with the wind. The looming clouds sweeping across the horizon posed a threat to the sun's glow, but it didn't matter, the sun's rays were bright enough to shine through the shadow.

"So, are you finally feeling better?" Finn gave me a punch to the shoulder.

I nodded slowly before turning to him. "I'm alright, I guess. It just sucks I got sick when Pam was home. I blame the late night park party." I fixed my expression so it looked like I was disappointed.

But Finn didn't buy it. He stared at me for a few long seconds, calculating my answer as he tried to fight through my web of lies. After a moment, he shrugged and settled back into his seat. I exhaled a breath of relief but drew it back in almost immediately as a sudden inferno scorched the inside of my head. My teeth clenched together and my jaw locked tight. The fire intensified and I feared my quivering body would give everything away.

And then everything stopped. The burning sensation disappeared and my muscles relaxed. Everything happened in a matter of seconds, but to me, the pain seemed to last much longer. The collar of my shirt was drenched with sweat. I rubbed the shock out of my eyes.

My health didn't improve much when Finn and I got back to our dorm room. I wanted to keep the organization like last semester but Finn wanted a change. I assumed he wanted the bed by the window so I agreed to flip for it. Finn rummaged his pants for a quarter.

He smiled devilishly. "Call it in the air!" He flicked the coin in the air.

"Tails."

Finn let the coin hit the floor and to my disdain it turned out to be heads. I caught his eye, and he winked. I, on the other hand, was displeased. I set my watch back twenty seconds and jabbed the red button, cutting his celebration short.

"Call it in the air!" Finn flicked the coin.

"Heads," I said, confidently.

The quarter fell to the floor and revealed our founding father, George Washington. I caught Finn's eye again and this time, I winked. He glowered and cursed under his breath. I couldn't help but chuckle as I moved my belongings to the window bed. He looked like he wanted to argue, but once I took out my stuff, he sighed in defeat.

As we walked over to the dining hall an hour later, my mind felt numb and my spirits at a crushing low. I felt like my physical state was getting considerably weaker, but even still, that was nothing compared to how dead I felt on the inside. I couldn't stop the thought of Pam with her boyfriend. Why she didn't pick me?

"So...another semester. Excited?" Finn propped up his pillow after we returned.

"Yeah, I guess."

I complained to Finn about the classes I was taking this semester—another English course, Western Civilization, Geology, and Business Economics. He grunted, telling me not to worry about it, and that my workload wasn't so bad.

"I don't know...I want time to socialize too."

"Like I said," Finn repeated. "Don't worry about it."

I didn't meet his eyes, wondering if Finn had any clue of what was going on.

"When's the next party?" I changed the topic. "Isn't there one like every Friday?"

While Finn deliberated my questions, I stood up and dragged myself to the bathroom to glance at my reflection in the mirror. Although my sleep cycle was about eight hours a night, there were dark circles underneath my eyes. I exhaled sharply, thinking that one day the torment inflicted on my body would be worth it, that the hardship would pay off and everything I desired would be mine. With a sigh I switched off the bathroom light and jumped back in bed. I pushed the thoughts of my deteriorating body out of my mind and focused on what Finn had to say about the upcoming party. The next one was supposedly in a couple weeks so that managed to lift my mood, just slightly.

Halfway into the night I jumped out of my sleep. My airflow was constricted, making my breathing heavy and unnatural. I cupped my forehead as sweat broke from it. I traced my face with my fingers, feeling moisture on my cheeks and chin. I drew in a breath before realizing it wasn't sweat on my cheeks but tears. I lay back down, dried my face and tried recalling what my dream was about.

I grumbled to myself. Everything was fuzzy. What I could recollect didn't piece together. It was like having multiple pieces from different puzzles, but one thing I did remember was that Pam was the exposition, climax, and resolution of my dream. I sighed deeply and tried to fall asleep again, but it was effortless, my mind was racing too fast for my body to slow down. I spent the rest of night glowering at the clock, counting down until the first beams of light interrupted my gaze. I got up slowly and retreated to the restroom, undressed and climbed into the shower, letting the water run over me, cleansing me of last night's toxic thoughts.

I shook my head.

Thinking about Pam shouldn't be poison to me. It should never come to that. If I get a girlfriend this semester, then we both could be happy, I tried to convince myself.

I shook my head again. No matter how many times I said it, deep down I only wanted Pam to be my girlfriend.

The rest of the week flew by in a blur. Maybe it was the lack of sleep that kept me in a daze, but I didn't mind. Lectures weren't important to me—I just needed to know what was on the exams to ace the class. But on the same note, the sudden insomnia episode was probably initiated by fear. They say dreams come to life through subconscious thoughts and desires, so if I wanted Pam that bad when I was awake, it was probably worse when I had no control in my sleep. But that wasn't the only concern I had. Lately, Finn had been acting different towards me. Maybe it was the stress of his classes, or worse, maybe he suspected something unnatural regarding me.

My suspicions of the latter theory were made sound later that night.

"How are you doing it?" Finn said suddenly from his bed.

I glanced up from my Economics book. "What?"

"You heard me." His tone grew fierce. Finn's expression was cold. His nose wrinkled, and his eyebrows were narrowing dangerously.

I chuckled. "Heard what?" I feigned innocence.

I returned my gaze to the textbook but couldn't continue reading. My mind was running with new thoughts, calculating the next best course of action.

"Don't play dumb with me, Blake," Finn said after a pause. "I can't figure out how you're doing it...and I don't mean to pry but as your best friend, don't I deserve to know?"

I sighed deeply and cracked my neck. "Really man, I have no idea what you're talking about." I sighed again.

He scoffed. "So you're telling me that you're able to ace every class and still find enough time to eat, sleep, and go to parties?"

"Yeah, why d—"

"It's just doesn't seem plausible that you're able to do all that...party with girls and sleep as much as you do!" He growled, frustration roaring inside of him like a caged animal.

"That's just how it is."

His eyes widened and his mouth gaped as if ready to argue but he abruptly stopped. I drew focus back into my Economics book and tried my best to simmer down the building anger as Finn cursed under his breath.

When I woke the next morning, his bed was empty. He didn't have class till later in the afternoon so I spent a moment wondering where he was off to. But that moment ended quickly and I ceased to care. My heart gave a terrible jolt as I realized Finn could start asking questions. I mean, he was a genius after all; it wouldn't be hard for him to connect everything together, that is, if he found the right pieces.

I sank into my pillow. My fists clenched together and I pummeled my bed in a fit of rage.

How could I have been so careless?

Were the mistakes in my behavior so noticeable?

But the most important question I had to ask myself was how I was going to fix this. I had to destroy all accusations and make Finn come to terms with my sudden awakening of intelligence.

Geology wasn't the most interesting class, if anything—it was on the other end of the spectrum. But one thing it accomplished was plummeting my already rock-bottom mood. The professor droned on and on about igneous rocks. I couldn't bring my eyes to concentrate or my ears to comprehend the lecture. I leaned my head against the desk, wondering to what extent my knowledge of rocks would serve me in the future except for maybe deciding which would best split my head open as punishment for taking this class.

• • •

During the next few weeks, the awkwardness between Finn and I did not lift. It swept through our meals, it seeped into our study sessions, and hindered our daily conversations. It soon came to a point where the silence between us became normal, a habit that had formed out of thin air.

"I'm hungry, you want to get some dinner?" I asked one night in our room.

He couldn't look me in the eye, apparently his textbook was more important.

"Nope I'm good," he said finally.

I scoffed and jumped to my feet. "Alright well if you're hungry and you want anything let me know."

He didn't reply.

I waited around for a moment, half-hoping he would change his mind and join me, but hoping was pointless. I left the room in a flash, hurried across the grass, and into the dining hall. I paid for two slices of pizza and sat at an empty table. I ate quietly scowling at myself for my inability to make friends out of random people.

"Hey, is anyone sitting here?" someone chimed beside me.

I glanced up. A girl I recognized from my history class stood there. She usually sat somewhere in the front, my eyes always caught a glimpse of her wavy brown hair as I passed by.

When I didn't reply, she asked again. My cheeks burned and my lips parted on their own, "Sorry. No, take a seat."

She flashed a small smile and sat with her bowl of noodle soup. "I know this might sound kind of stupid but... what's your name?"

I swallowed. "It's uh, Blake Dawson...and yours?"

"Judy Walker."

We spent the remainder of dinnertime talking about our classes, cracking jokes and complaining about the workload. I couldn't remember the last time I laughed so hard. But before our conversation could branch off to different topics, her phone vibrated and she had to go.

"Thanks for the company, Blake. It was nice meeting you." Judy stood up from her seat.

"Yeah, you too," I said dryly.

She paced away but suddenly turned back. "Hey, if you're not doing anything this weekend, my friend is having a party. You should stop by." She smiled again.

I nodded. Judy giggled and took out a pen and paper from her bag and scribbled the address. She handed it to me and hurried off. I clutched the paper tightly and smiled to myself.

I walked numbly back to my dorm, taking in long strides of air while doing so. I wondered if I should invite Finn to accompany me. I stopped at the front steps and thought for a moment. In the end I figured it would be better if I took initiative. If he chose not to show any effort, then the blame would be on him, not me.

I went in casually, meeting his eyes for a split second. Still, he didn't utter a word. He crouched over his desk again and I had to wrench my body towards him. My stomach flipped as I poked his shoulder. "Hey man, what are you doing this weekend?"

"I don't know, nothing?"

I stepped back, bewildered by his hostility.

"Why do you ask?" He sighed, turning his chair in my direction.

I shrugged. "I met one of my classmates during dinner and she invited us to a party over the weekend. Could be fun." My tone came out more relaxed now.

"Um, I'll see." He spun his chair back.

I marched back towards my bed and sighed. Although I was content that I made the first move, a sinking feeling in my chest told me things would never be the same until I told him the truth. But could I—or a better question was, should I—tell him the truth?

I shook my head.

No one else should know about Time Waver. This power was meant for me and only me. I began to feel better about myself again, I was able to let loose at parties and still get top grades. What more can I ask for?

I waited anxiously for the weekend. Finn hadn't mentioned the party and I didn't know whether or not he would go. I assumed not when the clock struck midnight. I left the dorm by myself and walked briskly under the night, my gaze wandering around looking for the lights of the party. I spotted a few girls turning at the fork and hurried over. Sure enough, the house seemed alive. I drew in a couple of quick breaths before stepping through the door. I scanned the room, flickering from one passed-out body to another. I maneuvered around the house, stepping over drained kegs and empty bottles. Instinctively, I searched for Judy and found her in a dark corner of the room.

But she wasn't alone.

Besides her own hands, there was another pair wrapped around her waist.

I was shocked, almost frozen, as I stood there and gaped at her. They were kissing passionately. I watched for another moment, rolled my eyes, and turned away. I groaned, debating whether or not it would be best to leave. That thought almost won over my rationality until someone grabbed my shoulder, forcing my head to whip around. It wasn't anyone familiar.

"Take a shot with us, mannnn!" the stranger slurred his words. "It's time for us to celebrateee!"

"Celebrate what?" I shot back a little coldly.

"I don't knowww.... Just take oneee!" He gave me a pat and handed me a small glass with vodka filled to the brim.

I hesitated at first, but the anger of Judy leading me on took over and I grabbed the shot. I exhaled and chugged the vodka down my throat in one swift motion.

"You want another oneee?" the same guy asked, his eyes unfocused.

And so I did. Not long after my second shot, the tension left my shoulders and my feet bounced to the base of the thumping song. The beat shook through my body and my heart drummed along, everything in perfect coordination.

Random people passed me drinks one right after another. Without thinking, I drank it like it was water. I didn't know how much time had passed after I took my first shot, but it wasn't long. My state of awareness evaporated and my limbs felt numb and deadened from the inside out. But for some reason it felt good to feel dead inside, like if nothing really mattered anymore. All my problems, stressors, and complications had fluttered away and I remained in limbo.

I closed my eyes and swayed to the music. At that moment I felt neither happiness nor sadness, just a state of pure nothingness. And that feeling was true bliss. If feeling happy didn't come with a consequence of sadness, or if joy wasn't penalized with disappointment, then maybe, just maybe, those emotions would be worth feeling.

I woke the next morning in a daze. At my very first blink of the day, my hand reached for my throat, which was dryer than desert sand. I felt my forehead next, which was pounding as hard as a jackhammer in a construction yard.

I struggled to get up and it took even more effort to maintain my balance. My arms and legs felt flimsy, yet my muscles were constricted and stiff. It was difficult to move and I couldn't help but wince at every step. I found an unoccupied restroom in the house and greedily housed myself in it. I managed to twist the lock before my legs gave out and I collapsed on the toilet. I knew what was coming next—staring down at the pearly white bowl had somehow induced a gag reflex. I threw up until nothing came out and continued after that. Once I passed the bile phase, my body was purified of the poison and I forced myself over to the sink. I splashed ice-cold water on my face multiple times and tried blinking myself sober. It worked for the most part and I was able to fully distinguish my surroundings.

I glanced down at my watch. "Only 7:15. I have two hours before my first class," I muttered.

I took in a quick breath before exiting the restroom and deciding what to do next. I settled on taking care of myself and freshened up in my dorm room. Afterwards, I took a morning walk to clear my head. I was in a different zone as I breezed through my morning classes. My mind was lifted in the air, my thoughts in the clouds, and my eyes fogged with disappointment.

It wasn't until Business Economics that I ventured back down to ground level. My interest was captured when my professor discussed an intern opportunity at Sequence Inc., a worldwide corporation where he worked part-time as an analyst. I jotted the interview information in my notes and as I scribbled, a building cheer grew in force. I couldn't help but think this was it. That this was the opportunity I was waiting for. I heard of Sequence Inc., many times before, it was the type of conglomerate that had its nose in everything. The company had to pay well since its senior executives made millions a year.

I snorted gleefully to myself as my mind left the class lecture and began mapping out a plan that would ensure a good foothold in the company ground. Working as intern would only be good for so long. But I had nothing to be afraid of, with the power of Time Waver and a little bit of brown-nosing, my climb up the corporate ladder shouldn't be too hard. Soon I would have what I wanted: money and power, and with those two, everything else I craved would fall effortlessly into my lap.

9
Something New

I TRIED TO discuss my internship possibility at Sequence Inc., with Finn, but his lack of attention kept my words to a minimum. A part of me wanted to settle things by telling the truth, but the more selfish side of me wanted to cut ties—to leave him envious while I succeeded so he would regret ever starting trouble with me. And that side was growing stronger with every moment we spent ignoring each other.

My head rattled back and forth against my pillow. After a moment I sat up and looked out the window at the dusk sky. My mind sifted through the good times I shared with Finn and I wondered where along down the chain of memories did his suspicion about me begin to arise. First Pam left me for a different boy and now Finn wanted nothing to do with me. A deep sense of anxiety rooted in my stomach. The strong walls of our friendship were slowly crumbling.

But was it my job to fortify it?

Maybe that's just what college does, it forces you to grow up and focus on your future instead of being tied down to your past.

I heaved out a deep sigh.

I shouldn't be worrying about this now. The interview was in a couple days and I should be preparing for that. My thoughts drew to a close and I glanced down at Time Waver, the key that would eventually open the door to my personal success. I smiled once more to myself as I lay back down, pulling the covers over my head. My eyes grew heavy and my thoughts became burdened with exhaustion, so I allowed myself to sleep a lot earlier than my normal bedtime.

"So the interview is tomorrow, huh?"

It was midnight when Finn spoke to me for the first time in two weeks. I didn't answer immediately, convinced my mind was playing tricks on me. But when he raised an eyebrow looking for answer, reality finally settled in.

"Yeah, I'm a little nervous, to tell you the truth," I said, excitement building in the base of my throat. "But hopefully—"

"You'll do fine!" he reassured me, laughing as he grabbed a handful of potato chips and threw them at me.

I laughed, amazed at how the atmosphere of the room suddenly shifted, as if the tension between us for the past month was nonexistent. But I couldn't let this go just yet. I had to make sure.

I decided to voice that thought after a brief moment. "So, are we cool now or do we still need to talk about..." I couldn't finish. I averted my eyes and stared down at my textbook instead.

His chuckling died down but his tone was still playful as he spoke. "Yeah sorry about the way I've been acting. I think it was just the stress of school that got to me. I guess I didn't realize you were such a late bloomer and now you're ALMOST as smart as me."

I glanced back, narrowing my eyes in confusion. "Almost?" I asked.

"Did I stutter?"

We laughed again. I couldn't help but feel impressed at how easily Finn patched up our sinking friendship.

"Well, I need to get back to studying. And you should start getting ready for your interview. Do you have any idea what you're going to say yet?"

"Just planning on using my charms." I made a joke and thought for a moment before continuing, "I don't know what they're expecting so I can't really prepare for it. But I have a good feeling I have what they want." I finished there with a devilish smile.

"What is it that they want?" Finn asked, bemused.

"Whatever they need me to be."

I spent the remainder of the day hunched over my computer, researching all the ins and outs of Sequence Inc. It was an international corporation, so I stroked my chin, and contemplated what a kid like me could bring to the table. The only advantage available to me was my education. Business Economics taught me about finances and unnecessary expenditures with multi-national corporations, and luckily for me, Sequence Inc., fell under that category.

I woke the next morning full of heart. I thought, as I blinked away the drowsiness and inhaled excitement, that this would be the start of my career. This was the chance I wasn't expecting but was hoping for, and I wouldn't miss it.

I got ready quickly, throwing on my best suit and slicking back the locks of hair. I left my dorm and hurried over to a main street. I searched blankly for a yellow roof until one pulled into my peripheral vision. I flagged that taxi down.

He pulled into the curb and switched off the vacancy sign. I jumped in and told him the destination. Without a moment of hesitation, we jerked into traffic and coasted down the streets. I glanced outside the window, looking past the buildings, tress, and people. I found myself speculating, not wondering what questions would be imposed on me during the interview. I had to nail every answer if I wanted to land the position at Sequence Inc. A new cluster of nervous butterflies hatched, and flapped around tirelessly.

The cab came to a halt. I stopped my twiddling fingers. My heart pounded uncontrollably but soon corrected itself when I realized we were nowhere near the Sequence building.

"What happened?" I demanded.

"Traffic jam," the cab driver replied casually. "None of the lanes are moving."

"But I can't be late!" I snarled.

"Nothing I can do about it."

I cursed under my breath and settled back into my seat. Just my luck, I thought. I only had half an hour before the interviews started. I closed my eyes and tried to relax but my legs tapped impatiently without my control. The car edged along, too slowly for my taste and as the minutes ticked by, the tapping intensified. I sighed out furiously and opened my eyes, flickering them to my driver who couldn't dissect the urgency of my situation. He was humming without a care in the world while I was forced to be in a circumstance that demanded my caring! I rubbed my eyes and peeked down at my watch and then outside again, the traffic was still congested, going absolutely nowhere.

I exhaled all my hope and inhaled in defeat. But I had to make a change—I couldn't afford to miss this interview. It didn't take long for me to make up my mind and I quickly set Time Waver to an hour previous, where I would be right before stepping into the cab. I pressed the red button and jumped back to when the taxi pulled into the curb.

I tapped on the window and the driver rolled it down.

I smiled. "Sorry, my mistake." I grinned wider.

The driver's nose wrinkled in disgust and screeched the tires away from me. I shrugged and wondered where to go from here. In the end, I figured the subway would be the best bet. It was a pretty far walk to the station but it sure as hell beat being stuck in traffic. Not wanting to bury myself in sweat, I settled on a power-walk to the closest subway entrance.

After buying a ticket and pushing my way into the transit car, I searched for an empty seat, finding one by the door. I made a dash for it but going so fast had blind-sided me from anyone else trying to get the seat. My acceleration crashed into a small figure at the very last second, our heads knocking into each other like coconuts.

"Hey, watch where you're going!" the person snapped at me.

"Same goes for you…" I winced.

The person that ran into me was a girl, probably around my age, give or take a year. Everyone's eyes bored into us. Their expressions showed nothing but surprise. But the girl in front of me recaptured my attention.

She threw me a fierce look, her slender fingers tracing the little bump on her forehead.

I gave her a weak smile. "Are you okay?" I said as my gaze roamed her face. "Sorry… I didn't know you wanted the seat too."

We exchanged another look before laughing. It was a half-embarrassed, half-awkward kind of laugh.

"Well, anyways, I'm Kristen Herter." Her voice was light now, not a glint of anger left in it.

"Blake Dawson, nice to meet you." I shook her hand.

"Seat's still open," she noted, nudging her head towards the open spot we were fighting for.

My eyes flickered to the seat and then to her, "I'm good, you can take it."

"I'm fine, please, I insist!"

"I insist harder."

Her lips pouted out but she did as I said. I grinned widely as a wave of satisfaction hit me. Even though I lost the seat, it seemed like I ended up victorious.

"What part of town are you from, Blake?" Kristen asked.

"I'm actually from New York, I live on campus at Brown."

"Wait. You go to Brown?"

I tilted my head sideways out of confusion. "Yeah, why?"

"No reason." She sounded like she was impressed which, in turn, made me grin wider.

"And you?" I said after a moment, flipping the spotlight on her now. I didn't know why but a flame of curiosity had ignited in my throat and escaped through my parted lips. "Do you go to school?"

She looked thoughtful for a moment, thinking of the best way to phrase her answer, I guessed. "I'm working at a small coffee shop right now, saving up to go to acting school."

"You want to become an actress?" I asked.

"You don't think I can do it?"

"No, of course you can do it!"

I wondered why she got so defensive, but it was kind of cute, I had to admit. I spent the remainder of the ride talking to Kristen. On more than one occasion, she slipped the location of her store and I had to wonder if it was intentional or not, but either way, I made a mental note to visit when I had the chance. Once the subway arrived at my stop, my eyes moved to the door and then instinctively back to her.

"Well this is my stop." I sighed. "I'll see you around hopefully."

"Yeah hopefully, and thanks for keeping me company." She stood up and furnished me with a hug. It caught me by surprise but I managed to curl one arm around her before she pulled away.

I flashed a quick goodbye smile before getting off the subway. As the door hissed shut, I pushed all thoughts of the new girl I met out of my head, knowing that right now, I had to focus on my interview and make sure I answered their questions nothing less but perfectly. I glanced down at my watch as I hiked up the stairs and up into broad daylight. I made a right and headed for Sequence Inc., which turned out to be only a couple blocks away. I still had roughly twenty minutes so I took my time. Pretty soon my gaze caught the sight of the towering building and excitement began bubbling inside of me like a geyser ready to explode.

I directed all confidence to my expression and calmly walked through the front door. I made a beeline to the front desk and politely asked where the interviews were being held. After memorizing the directions, I crept across the room, up the elevator, and into a broad hallway. A few doors were left ajar so I peeked whenever I could but kept my pace swift. Once in the waiting room it was surprising to see I was the only candidate here, which made me exhale out of relief.

Less people meant less competition, I figured.

I spent the time entertaining random and unrelated thoughts until a voice spoke from the door, "Mr. Bennett is free to see you now for the internship position."

At this point, there was no reason for me to believe I could fail. It was time to showcase my skills, talents, and capacity to this company. I rearranged my facial expression to display professionalism and confidently walked into the office. Mr. Bennett looked to be in his mid-forties, a stout man, with barely enough hair to cover the top of his head. But he seemed to have little patience because before I could close the door, he had already told me to sit down.

"Take a seat and let's get started," he said sharply. "So first things first. What's your name?"

"Uh, Blake, sir. Blake Dawson." I breathed.

"What's your aim here?"

I looked at him confused and unable to reply. I opened my mouth after a second to ask him what he meant but a voice inside my head hissed me to stay quiet. Instead, I talked myself up to him. "I plan on being successful in all my endeavors. I always put in my best effort and my nature is to never give up. I'm a team player and not afraid to work to achieve the standards I set for myself."

"That's not the question I asked." Mr. Bennett shook his head. "Well, let's move on."

I shifted in my seat as my anxiety levels hit a new peak. I scowled at myself and tried to jerk myself mentally awake. It wasn't that simple. A screw inside my head had loosened and was now rattling around, confusing me with obscure visions.

"So?" Mr. Bennett's eyes narrowed.

I gripped my forehead and concentrated on the interview. It seemed like a question was already asked but I wasn't aware of it.

"I'm sorry," I panted. "I didn't quite catch your question."

He shook his head again.

"Can you please repeat it?" I pleaded, my expression showing more emotion than my words.

"You should be paying attention," he snapped.

I gulped, nodding along.

"Why do you want to work for us?"

I didn't need a second to think. "It'll help me become successful." I replied.

He rubbed his forehead and I saw, quite clearly, that my answer was far from what he wanted.

"How would you handle the pressure and stress that comes with this position?"

I raised an eyebrow. "I can do anything."

"Do you have any previous work experience?" Mr. Bennett sighed loudly.

"No, sorry."

"Any previous internship positions?"

"No, sorry."

"Community service?"

"No, sorry."

His head fell down and he scribbled something down. I tried a peek but decided against it. After a moment he lifted eyes to meet mine, his expression showing anything but being impressed. I couldn't believe how quickly my foundation of hope had crumbled, the interview lasted less than five minutes and I knew it was already over.

"I'm sorry Blake, but I don't think you would fit in here." His eyes were cold. His words held no apologetic weight— it was only a speech figment of formality.

I muttered a quick thank-you to Mr. Bennett before moving backwards, making my way towards the door. My hand went for the knob and froze there, forgetting that this interview was just a practice one. I hardly cared how bad I messed up; what I did care about was how to fix it. I spun around and walked back up to his desk. I watched as his eyes slowly slid up to meet mine.

As I expected, he looked as if my mere presence was a nuisance.

"Yes?" he said. "What is it now?"

"If it's not too much trouble sir, do you mind telling me what I did wrong?" I said politely. "You know just for future reference and maybe I can work on it and try for a position later." I held my breath, waiting patiently as he contemplated my request. The seconds ticked long and it was a while before any of us said anything.

"Blake, when you are interviewing for a company like this, the most important thing to say is you'll do anything to make the company successful. All you did was talk about your own personal strengths." He paused there to take a breath before continuing, "You forgot to discuss what you bring to the table and what you can do for the company and not what the company can do for you."

I nodded, jotting quick mental notes.

"Also, it seems like all you care about is personal gain. Of course we want you to grow as a person but that's not all we want. We're a company and our job is to make profit. Remember to mention that you're willing to put the company first before yourself." He stopped there and thought again for a moment. "One final thought, you apologized a lot during the interview. We like confident people and repeatedly saying sorry is a red flag for us. And a strong firm handshake at the beginning and end of the interview won't hurt either." Mr. Bennett finished off on that note.

I took his words to consideration, memorizing his advice for me. My mind sifted back to the actual interview for a second and I realized I was just blowing hot steam, talking about how great I was and nothing else. My eyebrows furrowed instinctively when I figured advice wasn't sufficient enough, I desired, no, I needed a fail-safe guarantee.

"So, if I do all you said, will it promise me an internship position at this place next time?" My voice came out hoarse.

"Positive."

That was enough to assure me. I bowed my head and turned around, smiling wickedly. I stepped outside Mr. Bennett's office and quickly adjusted Time Waver to the beginning of the interview. I pressed the button and my body flooded away, washing back to a previous point in time. My attention was caught at once when a voice informed me that Mr. Bennett was free to see me for the internship position.

I closed the gap in a flash, wanting to start the interview before I forget all the pointers.

"Take a seat and let's get started," Mr. Bennett said. "So, first things first. What's your name?"

I remained standing. "Blake Dawson, sir." I walked up to his desk and extended my hand.

To my satisfaction, he gave out a low grunt and shook it. A hint of a smile stretched across my cheeks before I managed to control myself and sat down.

"What's your aim here?" he asked me, his tone still husky.

"To make Sequence Inc., money," I said.

His eyes flickered bright for a split second, as if amazed by my answer. "Why do you want to work for us?"

My eyes narrowed and the words came out in a flush, "Sequence Inc., is famous around the world. I feel like I have a lot to offer and this place would be a great place to start. It's a win-win situation." I fought back instinct as I tried to find balance between arrogance and confidence. "I've taken a few business classes at Brown University so a little fresh spurt of ideas wouldn't do any harm. For example, my Business Economics class taught me the basics of company finances, so I can attempt to look over the books and see if anything is out of the ordinary or unnecessary," I added.

Surprise painted Mr. Bennett's expression. "You're a Brown student?"

"Yes sir, I am," I said brightly.

He nodded his head thoughtfully, "That's very impressive indeed."

The rest of the interview passed by in a blissful blur. The second time around was almost too easy—all the questions he threw, I nailed them. It was almost laughable to see how many times his face lit up with surprise. But when the interview period fluttered away, the end result was completely different than the first.

"I think you'll fit in perfectly here, Blake." Mr. Bennett extended his hand first this time.

I shook firmly and flashed him a quick smile.

"Thank you, sir." I glowed.

"You'll be starting in two weeks. We'll call to remind you but just remember two weeks. Monday morning sharp."

I thanked him again before heading back the way I came. The journey home wasn't long but by the time I got back to my dorm I was worn out. I knew it had something to do with Time Waver but it was okay, my goal was accomplished. I marched in with my nose in the air. I found Finn straying from the restroom with a towel over his head.

We exchanged looks and he asked me how the interview went.

"I got in. Starting in two weeks." I grinned widely.

"Wow." Finn sounded impressed as he fell on his bed.

I did the same.

"So what do you think you're going to be doing there?" he asked after a second of silence.

I thought for a moment and then realized I knew nothing of the tasks I would have to perform. But that wasn't the problem, I could excel in anything using time travel... the problem was how often I could use it without destroying my body completely. Now that was the icing on the cake.

I shrugged and spoke my thoughts. "I have no idea but it doesn't really matter. I'll just have to adapt...adjust to the job. I mean, I'm going to have to if I want to make a career out of it right?" I took a breath.

10
A Wonderful Life

THE NEXT MORNING I woke up practically giddy. I spent a few minutes lying in bed recounting the past few days. I laughed heartily, believing that the puzzle of my future was finally coming together. But I couldn't sit around and rejoice forever; I had big plans today. I bolted from my bed with an excitement I hadn't felt in a while. I squirmed through multiple outfits, my lips turned down in dissatisfaction. With a heavy sigh I threw on a clean button-up and a pair of black jeans and took the bus to Kristen's workplace.

The coffee shop wasn't too far away from campus and it was situated in a nice neighborhood. Roads veered into neighborhood cul-de-sacs, and rows of trees shaded the area, creating a bubble of suburban paradise. The coffee shop sat at the end of the street and from a first impression, it had plenty of foot traffic.

Before walking in to surprise her, I flattened down my hair and brushed the dust off my clothes. I strutted in with my nose in the air. My expression was fixed to portray confidence and class but that was all external. On the inside, my stomach flopped around like pancakes in a tornado. Kirsten was cleaning a table with her back turned to me. Even with her apron on and her hair tied up, I found her looking absolutely dazzling.

I cleared my throat. "Hey pretty miss, how are you?" I asked brightly.

Her head whipped around and her expression glowed with surprise before being replaced with delight. I took it as a good sign. Suddenly, her eyes narrowed in suspicion. "I didn't expect to run into you here."

I shrugged nonchalantly. "I was in the mood for some coffee."

"Isn't there a place right next to campus?" She smiled at me triumphantly.

I cleared my throat again and humbly accepted my defeat.

"Well, what time do you get off? I bet you're starving."

She rubbed her belly as she spoke. "I get off in half an hour actually. And can we get something to eat?"

I rolled my eyes.

Kristen took it offensively and gave me a light punch to the arm. I snarled playfully at her before taking a nearby seat, allowing her to finish her shift without disruption. I let my mind drift away, wandering and entertaining several thoughts at once. I speculated how my work would go at Sequence Inc., and if it would affect my studies at the university. My contemplation strayed off from there and I found myself thinking about Pam.

How was she?

Does she think about me like I think about her?

Is she happy with him?

My eyes closed on that thought and I scowled under my breath. Since winter break I've been ignoring her requests to webcam. Maybe it was spiteful to do that, but it was necessary if I didn't want to hear about her and Bruce. I cradled my head with my arms and unwrapped my mind from those horrid questions.

"Hey, are you ready?" someone spoke above me.

My eyes flickered open.

"Are you not hungry any more, Blake?" Kristen seemed concerned now.

"Sorry, I passed out from starvation," I joked lightly. "Do you have any place in mind?"

She looked thoughtful for a moment. "There's actually a good pasta place a couple blocks away." Her tone made the suggestion sound like a question.

"That sounds satisfying." I flashed her a quick smile and to my surprise, she flushed a little.

We walked slowly, meandering through the human traffic. Although we could've reached the place in ten minutes, our legs had slowed to a crawl by instinct and we spent the prolonged travel time playing a little game of

Q&A. My questions mainly pertained to her life outside of work: her hobbies, activities, and things she enjoyed in her spare time. Kristen in turn, asked me about New York and all its glamour.

"Yeah it's a nice place to live and it never really gets boring. There's always something—"

"Look, there it is!" Kristen tugged on my arm.

I shut up after that, figuring story time was over. I opened the restaurant door for her before stepping inside. It was a small place, barely noticeable as it hung between two larger buildings, like a quaint little flower in the midst of thick trees. The server pointed us to a table in the corner and we took our seats. My gaze flickered around, capturing the entire atmosphere in one motion. It was cozy, a perfect place for a first date. It wasn't until Kristen murmured something that my concentration returned to her.

"I think I'll get the house special pasta," she said to herself, unaware that I was gawking at her.

I grinned. "It must be good if it's a specialty."

Her eyes trapped mine and it only took a second for her lips to pull up into a smile as she nodded, agreeing with me. I smiled stupidly and I feared it wouldn't stop. But I was saved when the waiter came, allowing the muscles in my mouth to relax.

"What can I get for you two today?" He pulled out a pen and pad.

"Two house special pastas please," I said.

He scribbled the order. "And for drinks?"

"Water would be fine."

He thanked us and walked away. My gaze fell on Kristen again and we stared at each other for some time, our lips parting ways as if we wanted to speak but were unable form any words. It frustrated me, knowing I couldn't keep a conversation going, especially on a first date, but to my utter surprise, she giggled.

"What is it?" I asked, concerned now.

She tilted her head to the side and looked past me, not at me but through. "Nothing. You just look so tense and serious. Loosen up, we're supposed to be having a good time," she chirped.

I couldn't help but let my lips tug up to form a smile. Kristen had that ability, to be kindly blunt while being graceful about it.

"What about you?" I shot back. "Laughing so crazy you're disrupting everyone from a good meal."

She glowered at me. "Wow, jerk. I would be offended if there was actually someone here besides us."

I whipped my head around and searched in vain for something to prove her wrong. But she was right; she and I were the only customers at this time.

I scoffed, "Whatever. I'm a person and it's bothering me," I said in an attempt to retain some dignity.

"Fine, I'll just sit here in silence then!" Her nose wrinkled. It was a joke but Kristen was glaring at me with an unsettling intensity.

"Lighten up, I'm just messing around."

Her lips were clamped shut and she shook her head defiantly.

I raised an eyebrow and tried a different approach. "Would it help if I said you look pretty today?"

To my satisfaction it was enough to get a murmur out of her.

"Only if you mean it," Kristen said sternly.

I leaned forward and peered deep into her eyes. "You look pretty today." My voice crept to a whisper.

Kristen kept silent. I didn't know whether it was because she didn't believe me or if I managed to steal her breath away. She paused and focused her attention in a different direction. Our waiter approached with our plates of pasta. He set the dishes and drinks down and retreated. Kristen's lips were slightly parted. I had the idea that she couldn't wait to dig in.

"Let's talk about how famous I'm going to become," she suggested. There was a small twinkle in her eyes, a dim one but bright enough to capture my attention.

When I didn't respond, she raised an eyebrow. "What are you looking at?" she snapped.

I dug my fork into the spaghetti. "Sorry, it's just your eyes," I looked down, mortified now. "There's something special about them." I stopped there, not wanting to add more fuel my embarrassment.

Kristen's face flushed a dazzling pink. I had to fasten my teeth into my jaw to keep from chuckling.

"Anyways, let's eat before our pasta gets cold," I popped the fork into my mouth and allowed the rich flavor to ride my tongue.

Her face grew pinker. "That's an excellent idea, Blake. Let's do just that," she sneered sarcastically.

The shift in her expression forced me to choke on small bits of food.

"So how's the workload at Brown?" Kristen asked as she spiraled some pasta into her fork and tossed it into her mouth.

"Iz prry gooz," I mumbled with my mouth half-full.

"What?"

I chewed quickly and swallowed. "It's pretty good," I repeated.

She nodded thoughtfully and kept her head down.

I took another bite. "Why?" I asked.

"You have to be pretty smart to go to Brown, huh?"

"I guess." I tried my best to look good without coming out snobby.

"Then wouldn't you want to go on a date with a smart girl?" She took a gulp of water as if she wanted to wash down the regret of voicing her thoughts.

I looked at her, confused. "What are you getting at?" My tone came out a tad sharper than I intended.

She jumped in her seat, a little shaken up, I guessed. But she recovered fast and answered with a question of her own. "I'm just wondering why you wanted to take me out?"

I didn't have to think. "Just to take you out."

She kept her eyes fixed on mine, her attention solely on me. There was no pasta, no waiter, not even a restaurant anymore. We were alone in our own world. I sighed, figuring my answer wasn't sufficient so I continued unnecessarily, "My criteria for a good date is more than just brains in a girl. I want a girl I'm comfortable with." I shrugged and took a deep breath. "I wanted to take you out simply because I wanted to. I didn't have to think about it, it was merely by impulse and that's enough for me." I finished my little sermon and trapped her gaze again.

Kristen's eyes softened for a second.

"Think you can woo me with just that? You're going to have to try harder than that." Her tone was light now.

I laughed gently. "Oh, I plan to."

Kristen let out a small giggle and we spent most of the meal eating in silence. It wasn't an awkward silence, but oddly comfortable—like the mere nearness of one another was enough.

"How did you like the pasta?" she asked once I finished swallowing the last bite.

I gave a little shrug not bothering to reply.

"What is that supposed to mean?" Kristen blinked as her teeth sank into her bottom lip.

I furrowed my eyebrows but couldn't keep the serious composure for more than a few seconds. The energy Kristen had was too much, it electrified the air, stinging my nerves, and forcing me to be happy.

"Nothing, I really liked it actually." I laughed, keeping my tone loose. "Thank you for taking me here."

She broke into a fit of giggles as the electricity grew stronger between us. I shook away the striking bolts and exhaled sharply.

"So what do you want to do now?" she asked, keeping her eyes on me.

I rubbed my chin thoughtfully and then cocked my head slightly to the side. "I don't know, what do you feel like doing?"

She mimicked my body motion and we sat there staring at each other. Suddenly a rebel strand of hair fell down that casted a line of shadow in the middle of her face. Instinctively, I moved my hand across the table and tucked the strand back into the layers of her hair. Her breath quickened. I should pull my hand back to a comfort zone but I couldn't, it stayed frozen right next to her. But when her eyes flickered to my lingering hand, I reluctantly wrenched it away and looked down.

"So..." I cleared my throat. "What's the plan?"

She bit down on her bottom lip again. "I don't know, let's get out of here first and figure it out then."

I agreed.

"All right let me go to the restroom real quick and we'll pay," she said.

My gaze stayed on her as she stood up and glided away. Once the restroom door closed I got up and went to the cashier. I paid for our meal and returned to the table as the bathroom door opened.

"Come on let's go." I nudged my head towards the door.

"Wait... What about the bill?"

"I already paid it." I winked at her.

She flushed a glowing pink. "Wow, really on your game, huh?"

"You know it." I wrapped my arm around her shoulder and led her out the restaurant.

We spent the rest of the day fluttering around, swooping into random shops—exploring the town. As we entered mid-day, the brisk wind turned icy and my body chilled underneath the clouds. Although it was a little too cold for my taste, I had to be thankful some-what—the sudden drop in temperature forced Kristen's body to huddle against me, closing the physical gap and allowing the electricity to warm us up. By the time dusk fell into the sky, I could say clearly, and without a doubt, that I was perfectly comfortable with Kristen.

"So, am I going to see you soon?" I breathed and checked around for a cab.

"Of course. Why wouldn't you?"

"Good question."

She gave out a small laugh. "Let's sit for a bit." Kristen gave me a tug on the arm as she took a seat on the curb.

"So how was your day?" I grinned as I sat beside her.

She looked down. "Good," was all she said.

I laughed nervously. "What is that supposed to mean?"

"Nothing, I was just thinking...how our meeting happened totally by chance. I mean, what if we didn't go for that last seat at the same time? Or if I decided to walk instead?" She paused, inhaling another breath. "Don't you ever think about that, Blake? I don't know, maybe it's just me, but everything doesn't seem to happen by chance." Kristen finished there, blushing a little now.

I shrugged. Her head flipped up and she threw a scowl at me. Apparently my answer wasn't satisfying enough to her taste.

"I try not to think about it. Even if it is destiny, I would like to believe I can shape my own future," I grumbled.

I glanced at Kristen just in time to see the shift in her expression. The scowl on her face was suddenly renovated into fascination. To the left, a yellow roof was just turning the corner. I threw my arms in the air and flagged the cab down.

"Call me." She scribbled her number before stepping into the taxi. I nodded and gave her a hug and a kiss on the cheek. Once the cab pulled out and disappeared under the night sky I hung my head. I entertained one thought. My meeting with Kristen wasn't by chance. It wasn't supposed to happen in the first place. How much can I possibly alter going back in time? Am I going to change her life too just by meeting her?

I shook my head.

These questions were beyond me, and even if I did wonder, it was pointless because no one could answer them. I got to my feet slowly, my toes freezing and my lungs out of breath. I blew hot air into my hands in an effort to warm them up but it was too numb to have any effect. At home I found Finn laying in bed reading. I gave him a nod and in response, his book snapped shut.

"Where were you all day, mister?" Finn asked as I changed into my pajamas.

"Just out...you know, on a date." My voice came out a little muffled. I pulled my head out of the sweater in time to see Finn's face twist with surprise. He leaped off his bed in one swift motion.

"A date?" He still sounded surprised. "With whom?"

I shrugged. "A girl I met on the subway."

"What's her name?"

"Kristen."

"Pretty name. So, what did you guys do?" Finn pressed me for details.

I laughed. "I'll tell you tomorrow. I'm pretty beat." I faked a yawn.

Finn whispered something inaudible and returned to the company of his blanket. I did the same, brushing my teeth and then climbing into bed. The moment my eyes closed, thoughts began to dance around inside my mind. As the hours flew by, I drifted in and out of consciousness, unable to sleep. I tried to recycle my thoughts into the trash, and empty my mind. I needed sleep; my body was getting immensely weaker, any rest I could get I should take.

• • •

The following days were unworthy of remembering and so I didn't bother. They were just dates on the calendar, nothing important. A simple routine of waking up, attending lecture, eating, talking to Kristen on the phone and sleeping, but the morning that dawned my beginning at Sequence Inc., was a day worth remembering, the sky was bright and the weather cold.

I felt restless when walking up to the front desk and asking where the new interns were supposed to go.

"Twelfth floor," the receptionist said without meeting my eyes. "Room 1291."

I smiled an awkward smile and backed away to the elevator. I made my way up to the room and knocked. No one answered. I knocked a second time.

Still nothing.

I twisted the knob and peered inside before stepping in, finding three people in a separate office. I assumed the man behind the desk was my new boss and the other two were my peers. I shut the door quietly and slowly moved my legs forward.

"You must be Blake Dawson," the man behind the desk said as I joined them. "I'm Mr. Andrews. It's a pleasure."

I gulped. "N-no sir, the pleasure is all m-mine," I replied, stuttering a little.

The man to my right introduced himself first. He looked to be roughly in his mid-twenties, blond ashy hair combed over in a style of professionalism. "I'm Timothy Mendel."

"And I'm Hank Smear." The other man to my left seemed to be even older. A good-looking man but short in height.

I cleared my throat before introducing myself. "It'll be great working with you guys," I finished breathlessly.

"Our agenda today is to teach you the fundamentals of this place. How we run things here and what is expected of you. At the end of three months, I, along with a few supervisors, will review your work and determine your value and future at this company," Mr. Andrews said.

At the end of three months, huh?

I promised myself at the end of the trial period I would emerge as someone important enough to be kept. I would do whatever it took.

"Do you have any questions?" Mr. Andrews flickered his eyes to each of us individually.

"No sir," we all said together.

Afterwards, Mr. Andrews took us on a tour of the building. He only mentioned everything once as if he expected his interns to have enough brain cells to memorize every company detail without fail.

"There will be a lot of busy work but I expect you to carry out your tasks diligently," Mr. Andrews said once we were all cramped back into his office. He seemed to be looking at me most of the time, like I particularly stood out to him. I thought it was a good thing but my mindset flipped and I questioned the sudden attention. It would make sense if the boss gave me attention once

I accomplished my tasks, but for it to occur right now, I couldn't help but be a little suspicious. Out of the corner of my eye, I saw Timothy and Hank twitch uneasily on different instances. My heart skipped, feeling like a black sheep.

"Timothy and Hank, you two both have your schedules already. Is that correct?" Mr. Andrews asked them.

"Yes sir." They nodded.

"Alright then, you can leave."

Without another word, they acknowledged Mr. Andrews' request and took their leave swiftly.

"We just have to settle your schedule, Blake. Mr. Bennett has told me that you are currently enrolled at Brown University, am I wrong?"

"No sir, I am a student."

He nodded. "It's going to be a lot of work and I can still recall the rigorous courses at Brown. Are you confident enough to be able to handle all of it?"

"You went to Brown, sir?"

"Yes, wonderful school." He smiled and I figured that was the reason for the unnatural attention earlier.

"Wonderful. And to answer your previous question, I am confident in myself and I just need one shot to prove it to you."

"The shot is yours." Then, after a second of silence, he asked for my class schedule. That caught me off guard. I was prepared to work around their time, and never imagined they would do that for me.

After the exchange of information, I learned that I would mostly be working on the weekends, which was completely fine by me. Before taking my leave, I thanked Mr. Andrews again for the opportunity. As I left Sequence Inc., the fear from before was displaced with a surging excitement, something I have never felt before.

• • •

I didn't know if I was losing my mind or if my busy schedule had stolen time from me, but either way, I couldn't believe it had been almost three months since I've been interning at Sequence Inc. Work was good for me, every task Mr. Andrews assigned, I took as my last, and that mentality carried me. If I did something wrong, Time Waver had the cure to that problem, and every one was corrected with flying colors. It was a good thing I only worked three days out of the week. Any more and I would've been forced to use Time Waver more than necessary—juggling school and the like. Sometimes I worked with Hank and Timothy, but more often than not, I found myself alone, struggling to find the recognition I wanted. And when I wasn't working I was hanging out with Kristen, putting in effort to make things work between us. Exhaustion was a common feeling now, but nothing felt greater. Being tired at the end of the day was a commemoration to the success I had built for myself. Life was getting interesting now that the beginning was over and the basics had been mastered.

11
New Direction

THE HOLIDAYS WERE nearing, and for some reason, I woke to find myself ecstatic to return home. I had packed the night before so I wouldn't have to rush this morning. I spent my time inhaling the sight of the glowing sun on the glistening snow. But the serenity of daybreak was brutally ruptured as Finn flew around the room throwing random belongings into a duffel bag. In the end, without my intrusion, he finished early so we hiked down to the cafeteria to get a snack for the road. The energy of the place was obvious. Everyone was dying to start their holidays and get away from the horrors of school. While the line was short, the tables were packed with roaring laughter and devilish giggles. Outside was icy so naturally, everyone huddled into small packs for warmth.

"Do you know when Pam is flying back?" Finn asked as he grabbed a bagel off a tray. "I wonder how she's doing with that Bruce kid."

"I think she's coming back tonight." I kept my tone indifferent.

Finn's eyes flickered towards me as I spoke, and then he chuckled. I assumed he was gauging my reaction to the sound of Bruce's name. It was true that a part of me still wanted Pam to reconsider her dating options, but what I didn't know was how strong that part of me was. I was with Kristen, a smart, funny girl whose company I very much enjoyed. So, why was it that I couldn't let Pam slip from my mind? Why was she chained down to my thoughts, incapable of letting her go?

When we finally left the cafeteria to get our things, Finns dad's car was turning the corner. We retrieved our luggage from the room and stowed it in the trunk.

"Thanks for the ride, Mr. Evans." I climbed into the back.

Finn chose to sit in the front since my father wasn't present. I voiced my wonderment to Finn's dad.

"He couldn't make it," Mr. Evans said. A moment passed before he spoke again, this time with an apology. "I'm sorry Blake," was all he said.

I didn't have the faintest idea as to why Mr. Evans apologized so I shrugged it off like it never happened. The majority of the car ride was done in silence. I glanced over at Mr. Evans a couple times and felt the tension rolling off him in waves. I narrowed my eyes, and wondered if I was the cause of it, but my rationality told me I was being delusional. I spent the trip gazing out the window.

Watching the snowflakes fall was somehow spectacular. Some fluttered around, following the gentle breeze and others sparkled, glistened with a coat of ice, but either way, they covered the sky with a beautiful elegance.

"Here you are, Blake," Mr. Evans said quietly but very suddenly.

My gaze flickered to him and then back outside. I had not realized the car had parked and I was in front of my house.

"Thanks for the ride again, Mr. Evans." He popped the trunk open. "I'll probably see you later tonight, Finn." I laughed, tugging my luggage out.

I pulled the front door open. "Mom, Dad?" I called out to the empty hallway.

There was no reply so I went straight to my room and dropped off my luggage before easing out to investigate. It didn't take long to realize they weren't home. I gave a big yawn and retreated to my room, convinced that taking a nap wouldn't be a bad idea right now. I was eager to lay down and shut my eyes, letting the relaxation of being home wash over me and douse me with drowsiness. My mind strode off and left my body disconnected and I enjoyed sweet slumber for some time.

Unfortunately, the sound of a door slamming bounced me awake. Feeling a slight grumpiness had me wishing I was still sleeping and I hesitated to leave my room. But it was my parents, and it was my duty to greet them, so I slapped on a smile and skipped to the door. I thought they would be happy to see me, but my hopes were dismissed. I've been gone for quite some time, after all, but at this moment it seemed insignificant. My mom gave me a quick smile before disappearing to the kitchen and my dad simply nudged his head as a way of acknowledging my existence.

I waited by the door as he followed my mom and soon the air was filled with fierce whispering between the two. I couldn't make out what they were saying, so I lumbered back to my room.

Half an hour later, I journeyed back and found my parents sitting at the dinner table, my dad's head down. My mom's gaze at him could only be described as cold. I tilted my head to the side as I went to join them.

"Hey, remember me?" I said playfully. "Your son, Blake?" I let out a fake laugh to lighten the mood but it went unsuccessfully.

My mom shook her head and my dad sank deep into his chair. My curiosity soon grew to confusion and I mustered up the courage to demand information.

"You should sit down for this, Blake," my mom said.

My gaze flickered from my mom to my dad and then back to my mom. But I did as she asked and went for the closest seat.

"So?" I started. "Is there something wrong?"

I didn't need the last question answered when I looked at my mom more carefully. Hurt was building in her eyes. It didn't take a genius to notice that she was putting in effort not to cry.

"What is it?" I asked urgently.

"Blake...dear...your father and I..." Her hands were trembling now and her bottom lip was quivering uncontrollably.

"What is it?" I asked again, this time more directed at my dad who was sitting there, motionless. "Dad, what is it?" My voice hard now.

"Your father..." My mom paused and looked over at my dad. His eyes suddenly fell as if he couldn't bring himself to look her in the eyes. "Your father..." She tried again, the shaking in my mom's voice intensified to the point where her words became incomprehensible sounds. After a moment, she burst into tears and I noticed for the first time, my dad didn't try to comfort her.

I turned to my dad. A snarl came growling out of my throat. His expression became alarmed and his chair darted back.

"What the hell is going on?" I demanded of my father. "Why is Mom crying?"

His expression shifted to coldness. "Your mom and I are getting a divorce."

I sat there and stared at him for a few long seconds, unable to register his words. I sank into my seat, shock riding through me as natural as air filling my lungs. I couldn't help but glance at my mom, pleading her to contradict his words, but her endless tears only confirmed it.

"Why?" My voice was shaking now and my eyes were on the verge of tears. I tried desperately to push them back, knowing I had to stay strong to make it through this.

My mom spoke first, "Your dad had an affair." Anger was fueling her words now.

Again, I was unable to let the words sink in. I wanted to fight against believing it but gravity forced it into my conscious. I threw a glare at my dad. "Is that the truth?"

"Yes." That was all he said.

My hands curled up into fists instinctively but I forced it to loosen up.

"With who?" I pressed.

His eyes met mine this time. "Your campus advisor."

"Ms. Terry?" I asked, shocked.

"Yes."

I stood up unable to control my anger now, "WHY WOULD YOU DO SUCH A THING!" I screamed at him. I didn't care I was spitting venom at my father. That was the least of my concern, because at that moment the image of my father disappeared and the man in front of me had reverted back to a primate.

"How can you even stand to be the same room as him?" I roared, looking over at my mom, "How can you just sit there?"

My dad laughed nastily. "Don't consider your mom a saint just yet."

"What?"

Blood pounded in my ears, my vision became clouded and I wanted nothing more but to go over and punch the man.

"DON'T YOU DARE TELL HIM!" my mom shrieked.

"He deserves to know." My dad's words were cold like his face. "After your mom found out about my one night affair with Ms. Terry, she went over and stayed with Mr. Miller." My dad leaned forward and spoke softly, "And now she wants a divorce for one mistake I made just so she can go be with him."

"Mr. Miller?" I whispered. "Who the hell is that?" And then the name connected with a face in my memory. "Mr. Miller, the divorced man with the two kids?" I snapped.

"That same one."

My heart sank deeper into my chest. My mom scurried up another batch of tears and buried herself in them. Then my eyes fell back down on my dad, who looked calmly indifferent to the whole situation. I sat there for a moment and wondered, who were these people that I called my parents? They couldn't be the same ones who raised me... they would never try to hurt me like this.

I have never in my life felt this horrible. It was like a hundred knives were pinning me down, each stabbing me clean and deep. My heart slammed around inside. I was afraid at any moment it would blow like a cannon and engulf me in flames. But even so, my legs twitched to move—to get away from these imposters and find my real parents.

Move, I told myself.

Get going, I commanded.

GET THE HELL OUT! My head screamed at me.

A surge of energy tickled my legs and propelled me upwards. I left the table and ran to the door, slamming it shut behind me. I ran and ran without a thought of looking back.

I spent the rest of the afternoon and evening hiding in the nearby park. The air felt damp and cold. I struggled to breathe calmly, my body felt like stone—impossible and unable to move. I felt a mixture of emotions, anger and resentment being the strongest. After my anger phase, my mind sifted back to when I first started college, how naïve I was to believe my parent's lives revolved around their sole child. I guess once I began my life outside of home, I was too focused on myself to know or even ask what was happening at home. If life was a game, my parents had already lost and were trying to bring me down with them.

I sighed deeply and then again in frustration.

I clutched my chest, feeling the worst possible thing imaginable. Self-pity.

"Blake..." Someone called out my name behind me. "I heard from my parents about what happened, I'm sorry."

I didn't have to turn my head to know whose voice that belonged to. I kept silent, hiding my head in between my knees, too scared and angry to face anyone. Pam sat next to me and wrapped her arm around my shoulder. I allowed her comfort to linger for a moment before something inside of me snapped. I threw off her soothing gesture and shot to my feet.

Shock streaked across her face. "What's wrong?" Pam asked.

"What's wrong?" I spat at her, my face heating up. "What's wrong?"

She kept silent, her teeth sinking into her bottom lip as her eyes slowly cast away from mine.

"You know full-well what's wrong with me!"

"I don't understand...what did I do?" Her voice drew close to a whisper.

Before I could stop myself, the words came out in a sudden rush, "Do you realize ever since you met Bruce you have completely cut me out of your life? We barely talk anymore...you said before you went to UCLA that things wouldn't change. But look where we are now...everything changed. You don't care for me like I thought you did, the only person you care about is Bruce. What does he have that I don't?" I stopped there.

Her expression was full of confusion as if my words had no backing to them whatsoever.

"Bruce has nothing to do with this," Pam murmured. "I have a different relationship with both of you."

"Don't you see, that's the problem!" I clutched my insides. I was speaking from the heart now and it was hurting badly. "Why didn't you ever look at me that way, why didn't you ever see me in that kind of light?"

To my surprise, she didn't seem all that stunned at my words. I asked her again why.

She took a deep breath and then answered, "Why didn't you ever make a move after prom, why didn't you fight for me?"

"How was I supposed—"

"You let me walk away, Blake, and I found someone who actually put in enough effort to want me in that way." She paused there, her eyes now cold and intense. "I am not cutting you out of my life. If anything you're the one who pushed me away. Last time we were back home together, you only saw me once. No matter how hard I tried to see you, you ignored me and casted me aside. Don't you dare tell me that I don't care. Look at where I am at this moment. I'm here for you now and you still don't realize it." She finished, hurt.

That caught my tongue. I had no idea what to say. For the next moment I just stood there, looking down at Pam, and her looking away.

"You..." I began and then paused. "You should go, I want to be alone."

Pam hesitated to comply, but after I turned away, she stood up and awkwardly patted me on the shoulder. "Sorry about your parents again. Bye."

I turned my head away, unwilling to look her in the eyes. "Bye."

At that moment, I realized I didn't care anymore. Her love for Bruce was out of my power and that settled it—life just simply goes on. Despair filled my insides, immobilizing my body with grief as my life simply fell apart in mere hours. The thought of rewriting history nagged at the back of mind, to change the fate of my parents. I heaved a heavy sigh as I realized that was impossible. There was a limit in place, a threshold of three days and who knows how long my parents kept their secret from me. I spent a few more moments at the park before finally standing up to leave.

As I walked along the empty streets my mind was occupied with one thought: escape. Not the same as coming back and dealing with it later, but the type of escape that required no return.

Yes. That felt like the right thing to do.

I set Time Waver back a full two days, feeling it was an adequate amount of time to fake a story as to why I won't be coming home this winter break. I left this time zone but not without glancing back at my house one last time. Tears streamed down my eyes before I shut them as my feet left the ground and zoomed away. The next time I opened them, it was to the sight of a dark ceiling. I sat up and almost jumped up in surprise when Finn grunted in his sleep. I leaned over the side of my bed and found my luggage sprawled across the floor.

That's right. I had been packing to go home.

I yawned as exhaustion crept over me. I half-glanced at the clock and saw it was a little past two in the morning. Suddenly invisible weights forced my eyes to close and my mind slipped out of consciousness.

The next morning, I felt tired but wide-awake as if my mind wanted to shut down but my body itched to move. My gaze roamed the room for Finn until I found him slouched on the floor hastily packing. I lumbered into the restroom, left the door ajar, and freshened up. But the silence of the morning was quickly dispelled.

"Hey Blake, do you mind if I pack some of my clothes in your luggage?" Finn squawked. I said nothing, still brushing my teeth.

As soon as I crossed back into the room, Finn asked again. My eyes flickered towards my empty luggage case, heart racing and I quickly contemplated. And then it hit me. I'll just use Sequence Inc., as an excuse to get out of going home.

"Sure," I said simply.

"Alright thanks. Do you need any help packing?"

I laughed cheerfully. "It's okay, I'm not packing until tonight after work anyways." And then I thanked him for his offer.

Finn nodded and his attention reverted back to his belongings. I dressed and set off, taking my sweet time as I took the subway to Sequence Inc. The building was always deadly cold, forcing me to draw my coat tight around my shoulders. I meandered through the crowd of people, into the elevator, and up to Mr. Andrews' office.

I entered the room. "Good morning, sir."

"Morning Blake." He grunted. "By the way, what day will you be returning?"

"Oh, I actually wanted to speak to you about that, sir. Turns out I'm not going home after all."

He looked up and gave a piercing look. "Why the sudden change? You were excited to go home before."

I shrugged. "Just not feeling up to it and I would rather be working."

My words probably weren't convincing but with the training I received at Sequence Inc., I was sure my expression was. Being stone cold confident, the key to proper business customs.

"That's fine by me. God knows how many people are leaving on vacation for the holidays so we can really use you on deck here. On the plus side, staying back will look good for your reputation with the company, Blake."

I couldn't answer immediately. I didn't want to work over the holidays but it sure as hell beat seeing my parents scream over the divorce. That was the important part. Who really cared about putting in extra hours at work? And like Mr. Andrews said, it's a plus-plus situation for both sides. I was on the steps to being promoted and Sequence Inc., had another grunt to overwork during the hectic holidays.

After work, I dreaded returning to the room. I took the long way home that night, walking slowly and, on one or more occasions, wandered around town. But it was only a matter of time before I found myself standing in front of my door. I pulled it open and fell into my bed.

"Long day?" Finn laughed.

"You have no idea."

"I took the liberty of putting some of my things in your luggage already."

I snorted. "It's alright. I won't be using it."

"Wait...what?" He hissed. "What do you mean?"

I sat up and shrugged my shoulders. "They need me to work over the holidays." I tried to lie smoothly.

Finn, however, didn't seem all that convinced. "But didn't you request work off, like a month ago?"

"Yeah, but I guess they didn't accept it." I dropped my eyes.

After a brief moment of silence, Finn spoke up again. "I guess I'll just see Pam without you then." He grunted.

"I guess so. Have a safe trip tomorrow."

A sudden yawn that erupted out of my throat put an end to our conversation. I hadn't realized how tired I really was until I was deep in my bed's comfort.

"Going to pass out now?"

I didn't bother to reply as I threw the blanket over my head as the light flickered away. I lay still, wondering whether Finn knew my actions were questionable or not. In the end, only one thought lingered in my head: never return home again—and not even my best friend can do anything to change my mind.

With the absence of Finn, the holidays at Brown were quiet ones. Sure, there were events around campus, but the dormitories and the cafeteria was emptier than what can be considered festive. I spent most of my time sitting by the fireplace, feasting on whatever I desired. I tried not to think about what was happening at home, but the more I ran away from it, the faster it came back around.

I occupied myself with reading ahead for my classes, a good idea that I never get around to. It was a shame that Kristen was out of town visiting family. I could use her bright personality right now. On Christmas Eve, most people would be at home, opening presents and having a good time with their loved ones. But I was at school, expecting no gifts and no company. When I woke that morning, my eyes flickered to my flashing phone. I had a dozen missed calls.

I checked the names of the people before sighing deeply. Most of them had come from my parents, one from Pam, and the latest call was Kristen's. I fought against the urge to return their calls, especially the ones from my folks. I sat back down on my bed and contemplated my next action. I buried my face in my hands and rubbed my temples hard, hoping an epiphany would come to me. I looked down at my phone, my gaze running down the names again until I realized I didn't want people who hurt me in my life. I'm sure Pam didn't want me to be a nuisance in her and Bruce's relationship, and I was definitely sure my so-called mom and dad yearned to start their lives over without hearing from their son, a reminder of their shambled marriage. I didn't know whether I was punishing them or myself, but either way my decision was clear: I wanted a new life.

I pulled on a pair of sweats and seized my phone off the desk. I dashed out of the dorm and ran to the nearby lake in a straight line. Without a second of hesitation I flung my phone into the water and exhaled sharply. Suddenly the power in my legs gave away and I collapsed to the ground. It was a strange feeling, almost euphoric. It was like a weight had been lifted off my chest and I was able to breathe freely again.

12
Another Step

THE FOLLOWING WEEK I kept myself busy without entertaining thoughts of home or family. I spent most of my time at Sequence Inc., working at a pace that was detrimental to my health but beneficial to the company. With the money I made, I invested in a new phone and more importantly, a new number. I was convinced never to trust the pillars of friends and family again, and for the rest of the holidays I purged my belongings of anything that reminded me of my parents or Pam. I wished to forget them, swap my memory with someone else, but I couldn't. The worst part were the nightmares that attacked my slumber. Just like a dying record player, I dreamt of Pam leaving me over and over again and the screeching sounds of my parent's divorce. My mind was weary but angry, knowing that life was cackling with laughter.

The following weekend I found my room littered with clothes. I spent a second swearing I had cleaned the dorm a few days ago, but that thought quickly dispersed as Finn groaned from across the room.

"Back already?" I called out.

Finn shuffled his feet before he stumbled out of the restroom with a towel wrapped around him. He glided over to his closet and got dressed.

"Yeah, couldn't stay there forever. Pam says hi, by the way." I gave a small grunt and Finn quickly changed the subject. "Is something wrong with your phone?"

"Yeah, I dropped it in some water so..."

He laughed. "Never knew you were so clumsy."

I shrugged and laughed nervously. When I figured the catching-up part was done, I changed out of my suit and lay down on the bed.

"Your parents miss you," Finn said.

My heart zoomed around and crashed into the sides of my chest. I closed my eyes and pictured my parents sitting around a fire, nodding happily to their significant others, regretfully their newfound ones. My heart sank deeper but I shook the misery out of my head. There was nothing anymore; my family was gone. Consequently, I should feel nothing for them.

"Oh yeah?" I snorted back.

"Blake, I have som..." He hesitated.

I looked up but I didn't dare meet his eyes, scared they might show emotions I didn't want to reveal. "Hmm, what is it?" I played dumb.

He swallowed and his voice came out quiet and soft. "I don't like keeping secrets from you and I don't know how

to tell you this... but your parents are getting a divorce—"
He broke off.

I didn't answer immediately.

"Blake, are you okay?" he asked gently when I didn't respond. "I know how much of a blow this is to you but just so you know, I'm here for you if you need me."

I spent a moment dissecting his tone. It was either sympathetic or pitying, possibly a mixture of both.

"So," I said finally, sitting up from my bed and trapping Finn in my solemn gaze. "When did this happen and why?"

"Maybe you should talk to your parents about this." His body jerked in an uncomfortable fashion.

"I don't want to talk to them, I want to talk to you."

"I really think you should talk to your pop and mom." He swallowed.

My head turned down. "No."

I kept my eyes on Finn who seemed to be in thought. Then he said slowly, "From what my parents told me...your dad had an affair with Ms. Terry. You remember her?" He took a breath and then continued, "Your mom has been staying with Mr. Miller ever since she found out..."

Hearing it the second time wasn't much easier. My insides still hurt and knowing it was public news only made my despair even more horrific. The look on my face must've alerted another intrusion to my feelings since Finn just had to ask if I was all right again.

I stood up. "No, I'm not," I said rather harshly, but truthfully nonetheless. "But what can I do, it doesn't concern me." I hid my grimace.

Finn nodded as if he understood what I was going through. I glowered at that fact. He didn't understand, my parents didn't understand, no one did. But even so, I couldn't help but feel a tinge of embarrassment as if their divorce was somehow my fault. It was irrational, I knew, but the feeling of disgrace was overwhelming, striking my rationality like waves crashing on the shore. I shook my head and it wasn't until I was back in my bed that I felt better. The thought of closure from my past struck me as I pulled a pillow over my face, I shouldn't allow myself to linger on this issue any longer. But it was impossible at this very moment, it controlled me and I couldn't think of anything else. Finn didn't bother me for the rest of the night, which I was thankful for.

The next morning was full of warm light, but even that had no effect on my rainy mood. Sitting in class, relaxing during break, all throughout the day I remained in a downpour. For the rest of the week I was plagued by the same feeling, the only change was the number on the calendar. Finn did his best to cheer me up but it was effortless, happiness was the furthest emotion I could feel. If there was someone who could come close to making me happy it was Pam, but she was across the country in Los Angeles, so I settled for finding joy in a different person.

And I decided to call that person.

"Hello?" Kristen said.

I paused, forgetting basic social functions for a split second. "Hey," I breathed into the phone.

"Who is this?" she asked, sounding genuinely confused.

"It's Blake," I said once I remembered I had forgotten to give her my new number.

"This isn't your number."

I laughed gently. "I dropped my phone in water so I got a new one."

"Somehow I'm not that surprised."

"So, you think I'm clumsy too, huh?"

"Maybe not clumsy just…inept at basic tasks." She giggled.

"Like what?"

"Like taking me on a date once in a while." Although her tone was light, the implication was indeed serious.

I hadn't really thought of treating her to dinner lately. It was true that work kept me occupied, but no matter how hard I tried to deny it, a part of me didn't care if she needed to be impressed or not. When the same thought echoed the second time, I felt sick, disgusted with myself. It wasn't like I was playing around with Kristen; the truth was that the butterflies with her weren't as alive as they were with Pam.

"I'll be sure to take that into consideration when you come back. Wait, when are you coming back?"

"In about a week! Miss me too much?"

"I miss you an adequate amount." I pictured her lips pouting out and the mental image forced a laugh out of my throat.

"Bad answer. If you want my forgiveness, I demand you pick me up from the airport next week," Kristen groused.

"Deal," I mumbled back.

The rest of the conversation shifted to more conventional topics, but it didn't last very long. After a few swapped stories the phone clicked and I headed back to my dorm room, where my bed waiting for me. I yawned loudly, stretching my arms way above my head before climbing underneath the sheets. I planned on only resting my eyes for a brief moment before starting schoolwork, but the next time I opened them, sunlight had drowned out the night sky.

I shot up and shook the drowsiness out of my head. I snapped my head around and glanced at the clock. I exhaled a breath of relief when I realized I wasn't late for work. The following hours at Sequence Inc., while copying reports and scanning documents for Mr. Andrews, I discussed the following weekend shift with Hank. Apparently Timothy had already requested it off, so it was between us two. It wasn't until Hank said he wanted to take a small vacation and go snowboarding that I remembered something.

"I can't work this weekend," I told him. "I promised someone I would pick them up at the airport. She's kind of my uh, girlfriend."

"Are you lying?" Hank said slowly, his eyes narrowing in suspicion.

"Of course not."

I spent the rest of my shift shuffling around the conference room doing menial tasks like filing papers and getting coffee for my superiors. I didn't particularly enjoy the grunt work, but if it was a necessary step to my success, then a false smile and idiotic obedience was a small price to pay.

"Another cup of coffee, Blake?" Mr. Andrews grunted.

"Over here too," a stouter man said.

Two more hands shot up and demanded the same thing.

I grinned widely. "Right away, sir." I memorized who wanted the drinks and quickly flew out of the room. Once the coffee was filled to the brim, I set the paper cups in front of Mr. Andrews and his business associates.

The corners of my lips tugged up to form another polite smile before I took my leave. My seat in the meeting was an isolated chair in the far corner of the room. I cringed slightly when the chair squeaked, but that incident aside, I assimilated into the role of a silent observer, inhaling all the business politics. Today's meeting concerned our company interests overseas and if this meeting went sour, our stake in England's market would be compromised. As Mr. Andrews and the stouter man shot words full of polite aggression back and forth, I watched their expressions carefully. Every movement, every action, every word, only fueled my thirst to perfect my own business etiquette. I didn't know how much time had passed, but by the time everyone stood up to shake hands, the moon was glowing in the night sky.

The rest of the week blurred by in a habitual fashion. The only abnormal thing was ensuring my goal of achieving excellent grades at Brown and a good standing at Sequence Inc. My body was getting visibly weaker due to Time Waver usage, but I had myself convinced it was necessary—that sooner than later I would have everything I wanted, things I could never achieve without power. As my mind sifted through these thoughts, I couldn't help but recollect the sacrifices that became inevitable. I wasn't too happy about it either. The idea of losing my family and one of my best friends seemed unfathomable a year ago. No one would doubt how much I loved them, but the future I chose for myself had no place for them.

By the time the weekend arrived, I found myself strangely ecstatic to pick up Kristen from the airport. I didn't know whether I was imagining it or not but I was experiencing happiness again. At times, I thought Kristen was the cause of it. Although I didn't feel as strongly with her, the fact that I needed her kept me attached. I waited by the baggage claim with a bouquet of roses. This wasn't what I called the peak of my romantic capabilities, but it was a good start. It didn't take long before Kristen bumbled out, following a trail of people. I took a right and swept around, my legs moving quick and silent. Suddenly she stopped, her knees locking in place. She glanced around probably wondering if I had shown up. I chuckled as I approached her from behind and gave a jab with the flowers.

A smile burst from her lips and she laughed out loud with relief. "For a second I thought you didn't remember to pick me up." She laughed a little.

"No faith at all. The point is, I made time for you. I am a busy man, after all." I grinned broadly at her.

She gave me a piercing look. "You had to make time for me like I wasn't a priority?" The corners of her lips now turned down.

"Why do you sound so mad? It was just a joke. Ouch!"

Kristen punched me on the arm as her frown shifted to a pout.

"Still mad?"

"Yes." She aimed another swing, but I was prepared this time. I grabbed her arm, forcefully released her fist, and curled her hand into mine. I peered at her expression and kept my eyes lingering on her face. I exhaled happily as her expression went from a grimace to amusement. Without another wasted moment, I presented her the roses again, this time her face went a scarlet red.

"So, what do you feel like doing today?" I asked when we settled into our cab.

Her head cocked slightly to the side. "I don't know… what do you feel like doing?"

"Already doing it." I smiled at her. "I'm with you."

She giggled, obviously delighted.

"I honestly c-can't think of a thing to do."

"Let me think..." I rubbed my chin thoughtfully. "There's a game tonight at school if you want to watch it?"

"What kind?"

"Football?"

Her expression wasn't as excited as I would've liked, but she seemed convinced there was nothing better we could do. While waiting for the game to start, I took Kristen back to her apartment to drop off her things and we ended up lingering there. Attacking me with a pout and a mouthful of snarls, I was forced to concede to her washing up and beautifying her appearance.

"I'm almost done," she snapped from the shower. "Just wait a little bit."

I went back to the living room, and made myself comfortable on the sofa. "I'm not trying to rush you or anything, but the game starts pretty soon and we still have to stand in line and get tickets and everything. Unless you don't want good seats?"

The next second, the shower come to a stop and low grumblings came from Kristen. I could have laughed out loud, but I decided against pushing her buttons when she was already agitated with me.

We arrived at Brown's stadium half an hour before kickoff. We managed to score seats in the dead center with a tub of nachos to keep ourselves occupied during the slow moments of the game.

"When does it start?" Kristen said fiercely. I assumed she was using that tone because the crowd's cheer was quite deafening.

"Soon." I directed her eyes to the field with my index finger. "See, the players are marching out now."

Kristen kept silent for a brief moment as the announcers in the booth came to life. After the introduction of star players and the opponent's team, everyone rose for the national anthem.

"Now please take your seats and let's get this underway!" the announcer thundered.

The crowd roared again as the players marched on the field, game faces set and ready.

"And there's the kickoff!" the announcer cried as Brown rocketed the football to the air and into enemy territory.

I glanced over at Kristen from time to time as she nibbled down on nachos like an eager little squirrel. I wondered if she even understood the game. I decided to ask.

She didn't answer. Instead, she thrust her hand into mine and stared fixedly at the field, which was full of players mashed together in a pile at this point. "I never understand why everyone just hits each other, it's like, go around him or something. Wouldn't that be smarter, Blake?" Kristen asked loudly when the game entered its second quarter.

I howled with laughter. "If they could they would, but it's not like the opponent is going to let them do what they want," I replied gently, sparing her feelings.

"Oh I see." She nodded. And then she turned to me, her eyes roaming my face.

"Is something wrong?" I asked, one eye on her while the other stayed fixated on the game.

"I'm getting kind of—"

"Look!" I cut her off unintentionally.

"What?"

Brown had just made a spectacular throw to its receiver in the end field, scoring an amazing touchdown and gained ear-blasting cheers from the home crowd. Suddenly Kristen stood up, hands on her waist and fought her way out the aisle in an ungraceful manner. I sighed heavily, picked up the nachos and trailed behind her. I caught the sight of her small frame heading to the entrance and ran up to her there.

"What's wrong?" I asked.

"Nothing, I just got kind of bored and wanted to explore your school instead."

I knew when she was lying, her nostrils flared up and her eyes didn't meet mine. "And it was getting stuffy with all those people, I just wanted a break."

"We can leave, you know."

Her eyes widened. "Oh no, I know you want to watch the game. It's okay really," She said, her tone light.

I exhaled. "No really, it's fine. I'm not a big fan of football anyways."

"Are you sure?" Kristen hesitated.

"Yes, how about we go back to your place and watch a movie?"

The look on her face told me a movie and cuddling boded well with her, something that was much more in her ballpark than sports.

Back at Kristen's apartment half an hour later, I felt dead tired and ready to pass out. I glanced down at my watch and nearly jumped up in shock. It was still early, barely the time where I went to bed as a kid.

"I'm going to change really quick. Be right back," Kristen called before closing the bedroom door quickly behind her.

I, on the other hand, headed straight for the couch and sat down. I switched on the television and flipped through the channels. My body went into a near-comatose state and didn't become revitalized until Kristen said, "Do you want to watch a love movie or a sad movie?"

She shuffled into view, holding up two films from her DVD collection. Her expression told me she couldn't decide and that burden fell upon me.

"Everything looks pretty sappy," I joked.

Kristen frowned.

"I think a love movie would be more appropriate right now," I said thoughtfully. "I don't really feel like crying either."

"Okay, let me put this back," Kristen zoomed off to her room again. She came back a minute later with a blanket in her arms and threw it over me.

"Cuddle with me," she whispered fiercely as I popped the movie in. I returned to the couch and placed my right arm over her shoulder. She threw her weight into mine like wet clay, allowing our bodies to mold together and make the perfect shape.

As the movie dragged on, I became less and less interested in the plot and directed my attention to Kristen instead. I chuckled softly to myself when she tried multiple times to catch me in the act of gawking. This went on for the rest of the movie and it wasn't until the credits started rolling that she turned to face me. We locked eyes and I suddenly became aware of the stifling heat in the room. Winter had barely left and it felt like California sun in the apartment.

"It's getting late, I should probably go," I got up, laughing nervously.

Kristen's face suddenly went into a pout. "I don't want you to go," She frowned again.

"Truth be told, I don't want to go either, but I don't have any clothes here and I really want to take a shower. I feel sticky and gross."

She nodded and looked to be giving up. I gave her a quick smile before retreating to the door. I pulled it open before she called out to me again. "What if you move in with me?"

I turned back around and made sure I heard right. Her voice small and expression hopeful.

"M-move in with y-you?" My voice came out shaking as I hesitated to give her a direct answer.

"Why not?" The shift in her tone caught me off guard. Before it was soft like a kitty but now it was surprisingly firm.

My eyes trapped hers and at that moment it felt like the right thing to do. Maybe I was being selfish, taking advantage of Kristen in order to say goodbye to my past. If I moved away from Finn, who is the only connection tying me to Pam and my family, then I will finally be set free. "Yeah, why not?" I said. "It'll take me a few weeks to get the paperwork done and be released from the dorms. But that's a good idea and it'll be interesting to have a girl roommate." I grinned widely at her.

Kristen looked completely delighted, more so than I had anticipated. I embraced her and gave her a swift kiss before bounding towards my present home. As I walked along the empty road, my mind and thoughts became happier and better, emotionally. The idea of having a new girl, a new apartment, and a new life invigorated me.

In the weeks that followed, Finn got on my nerves. He didn't understand that my problems were my responsibility and how I dealt with them was of my own accord. His persistence to make me talk to my family and Pam was that of an annoying fly, never ceasing to bug me. Every time we had a moment together in the dorm, I would keep myself occupied—unwilling to drag my thoughts into another conversation with him. But Finn was unrelenting with his nagging and I found myself missing his past self. The Finn who used to be aloof; the Finn who didn't think twice about the SATs; the Finn who didn't bother with any real world problems. Unfortunately, he changed and was now concerned for my wellbeing. He piled so much worry on me that the decision to move in with Kristen became a necessity. It was hard to relax and enjoy the dorm life with Finn hovering around yapping the same advice over and over again.

"Pam's been asking where you have been." Finn brought it up again one night.

"I've been busy." I snapped. "I can't make time to fly over there and see her, you know."

"You haven't given your new number to her yet," he reminded me. "You say it's a temporary number but might as well call her with it."

"That seems kind of pointless. I haven't even given you this number yet. It'll just make more sense if I give you guys my number when I'm done with this pre-paid phone..."

"Yeah, I guess that's true."

I figured now was an appropriate time to confess my desire to move out. I exhaled sharply and then started, "Finn, I have something to tell you." I waited for his attention to be grasped.

"What is it?"

"Kristen asked me to move in with her, and I think I am going to do it."

"Oh, alright," Finn said in a confused tone. "When did you guys decide to do this?" He looked suddenly upset. "I mean, it's a pretty big step, after all."

I scratched my nose. "I don't know, it just seems like the right thing to do. This relationship has to move forward, and if I want it and she wants it, I don't see a reason to not go through with it."

"When are you planning on taking your stuff over there?"

"As soon as possible."

"Do you need any help packing?" His face was ashen.

"Nope."

It was quiet for a moment; neither of us knew what to say at that point. The only difference was that I didn't seem to mind it while Finn struggled to find words.

"Blake," he started but broke off.

"What is it?" My tone came out colder than I intended.

After another moment, Finn found the courage to speak up again, saying, "What happened to you, man? You've changed...you've become a totally different person this year. You don't talk to Pam. Hell, you don't even talk to me. All you do is work and hang out with Kristen. I can't help but think you're trying to cut all of us out your life, like we have no place in it anymore, like we don't mean jack to you." He finished his rant, breathing heavily.

I stayed silent but a sudden urge to laugh consumed me, flowing through my throat and escaping from my lips and nostrils. "It's interesting you think that." I pulled out a textbook from underneath my desk. "Things change and people change. I mean, you didn't really expect us to be friends forever, right? We're not in high school anymore. I've grown out of friendships. My future is what's important to me." I thought my answer was sufficient, but Finn didn't.

"You can't be serious. What the hell did I even do to deserve this kind of treatment?"

My hand twitched unconsciously and I exhaled sharply.

"I've always been there for you ever since high school, you should know that. If there's something wrong right now, you should just let it out and we can solve it."

I rolled my eyes. This conversation was becoming less amusing and more annoying by the second. "Nothing is wrong."

"No, there is," he pressed.

My irritation towards Finn grew to a boiling level and I had to talk through clenched teeth. "Just drop it. That's how it is." My words came out with a growl.

"Come on man, don't do this."

It seemed childish but I figured ignoring him would be a better decision than hitting him. I flipped open my textbook and began reading about microbiology. A minute later there was a slight rustle over in Finn's corner and then the sound of our door slamming.

Finn had left in a fit of rage, and true to my words, I couldn't care less.

13
Curveball

THE NEXT MORNING I woke in a state of panic. Startled by the sudden attack, I gripped my chest and searched for a clear heartbeat. I tried to breathe evenly but it came out silent and irregular. I attempted to ride it out but with each second, the pain only intensified. Jolts of electricity shot through my body, sliding down my spine and stroking the nerves of my arms and legs. I wanted to cry out but I couldn't muster the strength to accomplish that. I reached out to stroke my scalp, but my fingers snapped back at me, as if they were fangs baring against their master. I felt life draining away from my face, sloping down and through my guts before vaporizing into nothing. The torture was becoming too much, but then suddenly, the pain receded, not as fast as I would've hoped but it proceeded gradually. I rolled off the bed and rested my head against the cold floor, sighing deeply. I stayed like that for a while, how long I wasn't sure…

Where did the pain come from?

It couldn't be because of Time Waver... right?

I curled an arm around my bedpost and pulled myself upright. I took another deep breath before reminding myself I had to get ready for work. But the morning presented me with a lot of complications. With every menial action I did, like brushing my teeth or washing my face, I winced in pain. My body had reacted badly, aching inside and out.

I was worried about my health and it wracked my brain all the way to Sequence Inc. On more than one occasion I asked myself if I should take a day off and recuperate. But I shook it off and decided to take it easy at the same time. To my surprise, the place was crowded. Bodies were flailing about, slamming into one another without a correct sense of flowed traffic. I had to push my way to the elevator, lumbering to the office. Everyone I past looked flushed and almost worried, which only made me even more confused at the commotion. As I twisted the doorknob, the booming sound of Mr. Andrew's voice echoed through the room. "WHO WAS SUPPOSED TO DOUBLE-CHECK THOSE NUMBERS?" There was a pause before he spoke again.

"What do you mean, I don't know?" Mr. Andrew's voice was close to yelling. "We're facing a crisis right now and that's all you have to say!" He slammed the phone shut.

I stayed frozen as he paced around several times. He looked in my direction and we exchanged a glance.

"Come in here, Blake." He ushered me in.

I bolted into his office and froze there, awaiting his instructions. But he was busy pacing, his eyes projecting a fierceness I hadn't seen before. Even from a distance, a person could feel the fury rolling off his body. Though it wasn't directed at me, the impression of smoke spilling out his nostrils was enough to make me nervous.

After a moment I spoke, "Mr. Andrews, I don't mean to interrupt but what happened here?" My voice was shaking.

"An idiot," he said, his voice coming out with a hard edge to it," made an error with the stock numbers and have just liquidated most, if not all, our company shares. This is going to affect our company drastically." He rubbed the spot between his eyes.

I bit down on my lip. "How bad is it going to be?"

"Bad."

That was too vague. I needed a clear-cut answer in order to make a good deduction of the situation. "Bad for all of us?" I winced at those words.

He sighed deeply. "Imagine climbing a mountain and when you almost reach the top, an avalanche erupts and now we're all passengers for the ride down."

I paused, allowing the analogy to sink in. If the losses were as great as Mr. Andrews described then they would have to fire a great number of workers. Piecing that thought together led me to the conclusion why Mr. Andrews called me into his office this morning. The losses were substantial and I was a sacrificial goat, unworthy of coming out alive in this mess.

"Who was in charge of the numbers?" I asked, as beads of sweat formed on the brink of my forehead and neck. "Is there no way to fix things now?"

Mr. Andrews suddenly turned to me. "The director of sales. My superior, Mr. Collins. And no, it's already too late."

There was a brief, but awkward moment of silence before my prediction came to pass.

"Blake, due to these sudden circumstances...we're going to have to let—"

"When did this happen?" I cut him off.

He stared at me with blank surprise. "What?"

"When did he decide to sell stocks on faux numbers?" I asked. My hands were shaking now and I felt my toes curling—a reaction to anxiety.

"Yesterday. That's why today is such a mess."

Ah, so it was yesterday, the same day I went to pick up Kristen from the airport. I could go back in time to save the company but I would break my promise to pick up my girlfriend. The answer was clear at this point, she would have to understand my priorities and how instrumental this company is to my success.

I scratched my head, knowing what I have to do but now, the problem was how far back I should go. I'm picking work over love but if I go back too soon, Kristen would expect me to be there, which means I would have to go back two days in order to plan a proper excuse. That should giver her enough time to find her own means of transportation home.

"Back to the point Blake, we're going to have to let you go." Mr. Andrews interrupted my thoughts. "I'm terribly sorry, you were an outstanding worker."

"Apparently not outstanding enough to be saved," I snarled.

Mr. Andrew jumped a little, probably from my sudden hostility. Ever since he met me, I'd brown-nosed him and that little outburst was completely out of character. With one swift motion I set Time Waver back two full days but a rush of emotion held me back from pressing the button. And then thoughts hit me, slamming against my brain like a sledgehammer.

It was their fault they're making me go back in time.

It was their fault they're taking days off my life.

It was their fault they screwed up and now I have to fix it.

Thoughts like those grew in force. It didn't take much effort for them to control me. It clawed down from my brain and into my limbs, tainting them with a burning fury. My hands balled into fists and without a second of hesitation I sent one in Mr. Andrew's direction. The blow hit him square in the nose and he crashed into his desk before crumpling on the floor, blood spewing down his nostrils and soaking his shirt like a running faucet. A sudden urge to laugh broke loose from my throat and it echoed through his office. I spent another moment savoring what I had done before my finger inched towards Time Waver. I grudgingly pressed the button and zoomed away, leaving Mr. Andrews on the floor.

My feet reset on the ground. I found myself sitting alone in my dorm room. I wondered where Finn was, remembering this was before I had the talk of breaking ties with him. But that wasn't important right now. Now, I had to inform Kristen it would be impossible for me to see her at the airport. With a heavy sigh, I dialed her cell and pressed the phone to my ear.

"Hello there, Blake!" Kristen said on the other end.

"Hey, how's it going?"

"I'm ready to go home now. Can't wait to see you."

I bit down on my lip. "Yeah, I can't wait to see you either. It seems like it's been forever," I said in a hoarse voice. I rubbed my forehead wondering how I should approach it. I decided to ease it in slowly. "So tell me about your day," I said. "Anything interesting happen so far?"

I stared down at my hands as she spoke. A part of me felt bad for paying little attention to her story, but I was sure it held no significant importance. Kristen rambled on for a few moments only pausing to catch her breath before continuing. When she was done she chirped in my ear, "And you? Anything new going on?"

That was the cue I was waiting for. "Yeah actually..." I sighed heavily before continuing, "Work has been really hectic lately and I've been putting in overtime just to keep up with their deadlines." I stopped there and waited for her sincerity to kick in.

"Oh no, are you going to be able to pick me up from the airport then?"

I sighed again. "That's the thing. I don't know if they'll need me. I'm sorry, I know I promised I would pick you up but with the way things are right now I'm not sure if I can follow through on it. You have to believe me, I miss you so much and I would do anything to get out of work." My last few words came out faint.

There was a short pause and all I heard was her breathing. "It's alright if you're not there. I can call a cab or something." Kristen was disappointed and I knew she was trying to cover it.

I would've felt worse if I wasn't worried about the situation with Sequence Inc., which was the priority right now. But I couldn't leave things with Kristen the way they were now. For all I knew, the damage I just dealt could spoil our relationship and sever my ties with her as well.

There was another moment of hesitance before she spoke again, "Well I have to go. I'll talk to you when I get ba—"

"I think we should move in together," I interrupted, blurting out my solution to the problem.

"What?"

"I think we should move in together." This time my voice came out firm.

"You don't think it's too soon?" Her voice shook a little.

"Nope, not one bit."

"What..." Kristen hesitated, her breathing coming out uneven. "Where did this come from?"

"I don't feel like I see you as often as I want to and if we move in together then I wouldn't have to suffer from that problem anymore."

"I-I don't know what to say."

"Just say you want to. Just say you want the same things I do."

There was another pause and then she said, "I want to move in with you too."

I smiled and it only took a couple seconds before Kristen giggled with delight. She started talking twice as fast about moving plans and wondering if her place was big enough or if she and I should start looking for a new place.

"Relax, babe. We'll deal with this when you come back, alright?" I said.

"Okay, I'll see you then!"

The phone clicked.

My muscles relaxed, and I was glad things were stabilized with Kristen. But that thought quickly dissolved and was replaced with my work problem. I bolted upright and rubbed my chin thoughtfully. First things first, I had to get the weekend shift from Hank.

By the next morning he had given up his shift to me with pleasure, even going so far as to saying he owed me one. The rest of the day dragged by in a lackluster fashion, but that night I was staring into a confrontation with Finn. I had changed the time continuum plenty, so breaking apart a meaningless friendship seemed like something I should repeat. Midnight ticked around before the door made a sudden movement and Finn staggered in. He shook off his coat and went to the restroom. About five minutes later, he walked out, his eyes droopy with exhaustion.

"How was class?" My tone was light as I buckled on courage.

Finn gave out a big groan. "I don't think I ever felt so tired in my life." I chuckled. "I still don't know how you do everything you do, Blake. I don't work and I still have a tough time staying on top of my course work. You have a job at Sequence Inc., and somehow manage to keep your grades up. And to top it off you're able to manage a relationship. Amazing." He enunciated the last word.

"Actually...about that, I'm planning on moving in with Kristen as soon as possible." My voice came out hard now. "So I'll be packing soon."

The drowsiness left Finn and was replaced with a mixture of surprise and irritation. The staircase had transformed into a slide and now we were falling to the bottom where we would be nothing more than acquaintances. Most of the conversation went exactly like it did the last time. If anything, Finn reacted worse this time around, probably because he was tired and cranky. He took me down memory lane with the promise he, Pam, and I made to stick together, but I just sat through the ride and waited for the end without saying anything more than a simple grunt. Finn was trembling by the time he ran out of things to say—guilt trips, stories, and experiences, everything we ever shared together—he threw back in my face. But I no longer cared about the past; my nose was stuck in the air and looking towards the future. It wasn't long after that when a familiar door slammed and the solitude of the night filled the air.

The next day at work couldn't have been any worse. Mr. Andrews wasn't present so I ended up following Mr. Collins around like a pet dog. He took me up to his office, which was located on the top floor, where I sat and busied myself quietly. I didn't know when he was planning on selling the stocks, so I had to make sure to keep an eye on him. A couple of hours into the shift, I felt my limbs trembling. At random times my gaze would flicker to Mr. Collins, who seemed disinterested in everything but his desk phone. The questions of when and what time preoccupied my thoughts, making me dizzy with anticipation. I figured as Director of Sales he would have plenty of work that needed to be done, but if so, why wasn't he doing anything? It had to be something with his phone. Was he waiting for a call before selling the stocks?

I couldn't have been more right.

When his phone finally did ring, he answered it without hesitation. He was mumbling fast so I fluttered silently to the door. Words became more distinct and my breath drew short when Mr. Collins discussed the company assets on the phone. I backed away from the door when my superior said he was going to "do it" and not a second later, his phone clicked and he stumbled out his office in a daze. I followed him, my pace matching his, but a few steps behind. I glanced quickly from side to side, my heartbeat intensifying as my adrenaline-filled blood coursed through and fueled my muscles.

"You have to do it. You have to do it," I told myself.

I positioned my left leg behind me and raised my arms for a quick pounce. I gave out a small growl and then launched my body forward, my arms slamming into Mr. Collins. He yelped and I quickly threw a hand over his mouth. I shoved Mr. Collins to the side with enough force that he crashed against the wall and fell flat on his face.

"I know what you're planning on doing," I muttered, almost growling the words.

He stayed silent for a moment, staring at me with a pair of hallowed eyes.

"You can't sell the stocks. You'll destroy this company."

His expression shifted to shock, "H-how did you know?" Mr. Collins stuttered.

"That doesn't matter."

"This has to be done!" he shouted, his voice scratchy with a hard edge to it.

"Tell that to the authorities."

I grabbed a handful of Mr. Collins' shirt and propelled him upwards. He fought me, but the boost of adrenaline proved his efforts fruitless. I dragged him towards the nearest security guard, who gave me a quick glance of confusion before realizing the situation. He ran up to us, hand ready at the draw.

"What's the meaning of this?" The guard's eyes flickered from me to my senior captive and then to me again.

I dropped Mr. Collins at his feet. "I overheard him talking about liquidating the company shares," I said a little breathlessly. "Not just some, but all of them."

The guard's face was masked with perplexity. Obviously this situation was sky-high out of his authoritative powers. Mr. Collins trembled beside me but I didn't know why. Was he scared of the consequences?

I scoffed.

After a few moments of muddled bickering, I convinced several guards to detain my superior for further questioning, and by that, if his actions were really in the company's "best interest". I sighed a breath of relief knowing that the person who put the company in jeopardy was now in custody. In one day I changed so much history that I almost felt regret.

I couldn't sleep that night. I looked over at Finn's empty bed for what seemed like hours. My gut told me the role of the villain belonged to me and my stomach churned because of it. But I knew Finn would be okay without me, and he knew it too. So now he, Pam and her boyfriend Bruce can live happily without my jealous flashes and intrusion.

Dawn came knocking sooner than I expected and when it came time for work, I had little to no rest to charge my batteries. I yawned heavily and walked into the sounds of a thriving business. The atmosphere felt different than the first time, which was a good sign. It was still chaotic but in a less post-apocalyptic type of way. I made a beeline to Mr. Andrews' office where I was filled in on my accomplishments. I was thanked for stopping Mr. Collins with a full month's paid vacation, a token of their gratefulness and which I can use at anytime. I figured I could use the break from work if my health ever took a steep decline.

"Blake, there's something else the company would like to give you." Mr. Andrews coughed, interrupting my thoughts. He gave another cough before continuing, "We would like to promote you to junior executive. Your skills and the way you manage a crisis are something the board and I see as leadership material. We feel you are ready."

My body went rigid with shock. Any words that wanted to be voiced came out mute. After a moment, I was able to regain control of my voice box. "They want me to be a junior executive?" I muttered out these words, my voice still ridden with disbelief.

"Only if you're up to it. It's a lot more money but also a lot more stress. You will be the youngest to hold such a position ever, you may not qualify in terms of experience but you have yet to make a mistake. The action you pulled with Mr. Collins has only reaffirmed what I already knew— that you were willing to go against a higher authority to protect the company." He paused for a moment and finished his speech by dragging back to his first point, "But only if you're up to it, Blake."

In a really strange occurrence, my mouth moved faster than my thoughts and before I realized it, I had already blurted out, "I am ready".

Mr. Andrews shot me a quick, confident smile before standing up to give me a handshake, a respectful way to seal the deal. The rest of the workday passed by in orderly fashion, but not without recognition. From being just Mr. Andrews' lapdog assistant, I was suddenly recognized throughout the company, and the emotions buzzing inside my skull were almost comparable to that of a celebrity. Every time I did a task, someone flashed me a grin and didn't bother to lower their voices as they discussed my triumph. It was a bit late to act modest and a part of me felt that the spotlight was almost...comforting, to the say the very least. It was a shame when the clock ticked five and I had to catch a cab home.

I was surprised that the feeling of happiness hadn't seeped away yet. I dialed Kristen and broke down my day for her. I couldn't tell if she was getting better at acting but she seemed perfectly ecstatic for my accomplishments. After catching up on our days, the topic flipped and we made plans so I could move in with her in a few weeks.

• • •

That period of time raced by at a frightening speed. With the extra work piled on at Sequence Inc., it had left me with more fatigue than usual. It was enough to make me reconsider continuing my education. Sequence Inc., made me a junior executive, which meant I had potential in the company's eyes. Brown can come later if I truly wanted my degree, but for now, my job was of utmost importance. But I didn't mind, I was writing my success story bit by bit—working late into the night, processing documents, going over sale reports, learning new business tactics—every little detail was bearing fruit for some other skill that needed to be harvested.

"Hey, babe?" I set boxes next to the bed. "Where am I supposed to hang my clothes if you have all the space in the closet?"

"I hadn't thought about that," she called from the kitchen.

"Really?" I pouted. "Am I supposed to hang my clothes in trash bags outside the window?"

"Whatever works for you, babe."

"Maybe I'll do just that with your clothes and take the closet for myself." I gave out a mischievous laugh that beckoned Kristen to come see me in the bedroom. "Ah, now you show yourself when your stuff is at stake," I continued before grabbing her waist and pulling her close.

Kristen rolled her eyes. "I was only kidding...I left you two drawers in the dresser, that's all you need, right?" she said slyly.

"Yeah, but I can't fold my jackets and dress shirts, it wouldn't fit with my casual wear."

"Fine, I'll clear some room in the closet," Kristen said reluctantly, before ripping out of my grip.

As she cleared some space, I unpacked the rest of my belongings in an orderly fashion. I guess all I really brought over were clothes. All the things that held any sentimental value were associated with my forgotten family and friends. Maybe I should have at least packed one photo album...

No. I shook my head.

I made my decision with them; their part in my life was over. They'd made their choices and I made mine. Plus, I can always start new memories with Kristen and friends from work, which reminded me...I should try to make some.

"So, how did your roommate take you leaving, that must kind of suck for him, huh?" Kristen said.

I didn't reply right away, or better yet I didn't know what to say.

"I think he'll survive." My voice came out with an edge to it.

Although the day was filled with painstaking memories, the night was so much better. Having the comfort of someone laying next me is so simple and yet it is the simplest things that make life truly worth it. Usually it would take an hour or so before my thoughts allowed my mind to drift off, but cuddling with Kristen put me into slumber almost instantly.

I fell into the park near my house and I found Pam sitting on the swings, gently swaying back and forth. I scanned the area, my gaze flickering around—realizing we were alone. Without my conscious telling me to, my legs trotted closer to Pam who, from my distance, remained hazy. My infatuation-stained blood poured into my heart, pumping it to an irregular beat. My breath quickened and I ran towards her. I wasn't sure if I was running backwards or not but Pam was moving farther and farther away. I pushed harder, letting the dust ride behind me, running as hard as I could until my lungs were at the breaking point, ready to burst at the pace I was taking. But I didn't care, I couldn't care for my wellbeing knowing Pam was so close…and yet I had to realize I could never reach her, it was too late for her to accept my feelings.

"Blake?" someone said from the world of reality.

"Pam?" I murmured without thinking. It took a second of realization before reality sunk in and I sat upright.

14
Winding Down

"I'M SORRY?"

"W-what?" I stammered. "I didn't say anything."

The area between Kristen's eyebrows creased as her mouth pouted in a silent but building fury. "I'm absolutely positive you said some other girl's name." The tone of her voice was even more threatening. "You called out Pam. Who is she?"

I exhaled heavily before flickering my eyes away. When I was ready to answer my eyes trapped Kristen's. "She was my childhood friend. We kind of had a falling out. And I dreamt about seeing her again. That was all." I exhaled again when I realized how much I missed Pam in my life.

Though it was subtle, Kristen's expression shifted to concern with a tint of guilt. She probably felt bad for asking such piercing questions about the life I left behind. Kristen really cared about me, I comforted myself with that thought.

"Yeah, I'm sorry I worried you. I never mentioned her to you because, like I said, she's not my friend any more." I paused, took another deep breath, before continuing, "It was just my memories playing with me." I finished there.

She threw her arm around me and spoke in a soothing voice, "Shh…it's okay, even if she's not here, I am and I always will be."

I accepted her sympathy and rested my head on her chest, listening to the quiet thumps of her heart. At that moment, the clock ticked and I believed Kristen's heart was beating for me and me alone.

"Why did this falling out happen anyways…if you don't mind me asking?" Kristen said after a brief moment of silence.

My lips felt chapped and I spent a second moistening them before replying, "Distance shows who is really willing to stay in your life and who isn't."

My answer was partly true. Although Kristen and I were in a committed relationship, I figured there were still facts I can leave out. For example, my impulsive and undying love for Pam was one of them, and the fact that she had a boyfriend who wasn't me was another.

"Well then, I hope you listen to your own words and realize I am still here," Kristen said cheerfully.

"I know you are, and I am so thankful for it. I don't know what my life would be like without you."

"You're being a little too cute right now."

I chuckled quietly. "My charm only comes out with you."

"Only for me," she whispered.

It didn't take long for both of us to drift off again—our bodies linked together as if they were carved in stone and unwilling to part.

The smell of cooking eggs and bacon drove my nose upward, and lifted my feet off the bed. I felt unconscious following the scent back to the kitchen. I rubbed the tiredness from my eyes and let out a yawn as I settled into a seat. Kristen caught whiff of my presence and set breakfast in front of me.

"I can get used to this," I picked up my fork.

Kristen rolled her eyes before digging into her own plate.

"So, what are your plans for today?" I asked, my mouth half-full with eggs.

"Um...I have an audition around noon, but that's about it. What about you?"

"I have to work, not sure when I'll be done though."

"If I'm not too tired I'll make dinner too," Kristen noted.

The corners of her lips pulled up, which forced mine to mirror hers. After a silent moment of trapped gazes, I lumbered to the restroom to get ready for work. As I brushed my teeth, there was something unfamiliar in the reflection. I looked closer; the eyes that stared back were foreign, almost unrecognizable. Wrinkles attacked every inch of visible face and black bags hung underneath my eyes. I ran my hands through my hair in frustration only to find another startling realization. The change was subtle but my hairline was receding. Panicking, I bent my arm and stroked the side of my cheek, my mouth falling into an inaudible gasp.

My skin was moist and clammy almost as if I was nearing my time, inches away from picking out my coffin and headstone. I exhaled sharply and forced my head to turn away. I sighed out in angst, wondering if my internal organs were just as bad. But I couldn't wonder for too long because just then there came a light pounding on the door.

"Blake, are you alright?" Kristen said worriedly. "Is it the food?"

"No, I'm fine. Sorry, I'm just washing up."

If I spent any more time in the restroom, her concern would grow so I blinked away the anxiety and slapped on a grin.

The rest of the day exhausted me. At one point I felt like collapsing. Maybe it was the stress of the promotion, but like with all situations, I knew I just had to adapt to it.

Right before a meeting, Mr. Andrews buzzed me to come meet him. Walking into his office, I heard him on the phone with someone. Once I drew closer, I heard my name multiple times. "I'll be sure to let Blake know—"

Suspicion bubbled in my gut as I wondered why Mr. Andrews was talking about me.

"Yes, yes. Definitely we can not have that." The phone clicked.

Next second, my gaze trapped his and he ushered me in. His expression was colored pale, almost as if he was nervous to see me. "Blake, the reason I called you is because there is a problem."

I gulped.

He hesitated. I assumed he was trying to find the right words to say. "Have you been to school lately?" he said after a moment.

I looked down. "Not really, sir. To tell you the truth Sequence Inc., has been keeping me pretty busy."

"Oh." He paused before continuing, "See there's a problem, the reason we admitted you to work for our company at such an early age was because you were a Brown student. We want you to continue to pursue an education. It'll look bad for us if you drop out."

I was confused, staring at him with blank eyes. "Who am I hurting with my choices, sir?" I wondered out loud. "My education is my decision."

His expression grew concerned. "Yourself, Blake. If you want to advance in the company you will need a degree. They won't allow you to pursue a higher rank without one. You have so much potential, Blake, don't let it go to waste."

"What happens now?"

"You'll be on a probation period with Sequence Inc. If things remain the same as they are now, your future at this company can be at risk. I suggest you get your act together. Go back to school and then there will be no problem," Mr. Andrews said roughly.

My face fell as I sat there wondering how I could juggle school and work again without using Time Waver. The answer was clear: I couldn't.

"If you need to be demoted to work less hours, I can make it happen." That was Mr. Andrews attempt at consoling me. A demotion.

"No, sir. I love my job. I'll find a way to go to school and live up to the company's expectations." I gave out a fake big grin.

"Then we should have no problem in the future." He grunted back.

I nodded and proceeded to stand up.

"Wait, Blake, there's one more thing."

I tilted my head to the side. "Did I do something else, sir?" I didn't mean to sound snappy but I couldn't help the way it came out.

"No, there's an executive party here next Saturday. I think it would be a good opportunity for you to meet some corporate heads and connect."

My expression lit up and the harshness in my voice vanished. "Really? That would be great!"

"Bring someone if you want to, I'll put you on the guest list with a plus one."

Afterwards, I left and traveled down the elevator. I went back to work with a half-full heart. On one hand, I'll be meeting the head honchos of the company and hopefully pull off a good impression, but on the other hand, I had to worry about school and grades again. I groaned and threw my hands over my eyes. My life was going exactly as I had planned. So why was I unhappy? I knew I would come across this question again in the future but for now, work came first and my happiness was a far-off second.

I returned to the apartment only to be engrossed in a euphoric aroma. I found Kristen in the kitchen, her hand gently stirring what I assumed to be a pot of stew.

"Dinner should be ready soon!" She welcomed me.

"It smells delicious. By the way, what are you doing next weekend?" I pulled the coat off my shoulders and draped it on the couch.

Kristen tilted her head thoughtfully to the side. "Spending it with you, what else would I be doing?" she chirped.

I laughed gently before wrapping my arms around her waist. She pushed her index finger against my chest, grazing it up and down in a repetitive fashion.

"Why?" she pressed. "Do you have something in mind?"

"There's a company party I have to attend and I was wondering if you would go with me."

I noticed a slight fall in her expression but she recovered quickly. "That sounds fun." She smiled. "Sure, I'll be your date."

I gave Kristen a swift kiss. "Great, I'll have the hottest girl in the room then."

A small smile broke from her lips before she steered me into a seat, prepping me for a hot meal. Later that night, as Kristen was on the phone with her parents, I used the time to prepare my re-admittance to Brown. After a long moment her presence became distinguished and she rushed to the bed. She jumped underneath the covers, grabbed my arm and draped it around her.

I raised an eyebrow, but before I could speak she beat me to it. "Shut up, just cuddle." She pouted, her nose wrinkling in the process.

"I can't ask what's wrong?"

Her head flared up. "It's my parents... they want me to attend my cousin's wedding with them."

"Wow, how could they ask that of you? Its utterly unforgivable for them to make such a request of their daughter!" I said, sarcastically.

Kristen took my humor and returned it with a playful punch.

"No seriously, I don't understand what's wrong."

"It's nothing really. I just don't really like spending time with my family or my extended family, for that matter."

"Any reason why that is?" I gripped her shoulder.

Kristen sighed. "I was the oddball, choosing to go into acting instead of a safer route in life."

"That's why I admire you," I said.

She stared up at me, her eyes twinkling again. "But anyways, it's next weekend."

My mouth twitched. "But next Saturday is my company party."

"I know, I'll go to that and then fly to the wedding afterwards." She kissed me on the cheek.

"You don't have to. It's okay if you want to go to the wedding early!" I insisted.

She giggled. "Trust me, I'll use any excuse to spend less time with my family."

This time I kissed her. "Well then, I'll drop you off at the airport myself."

"I'd expect nothing less from my boyfriend."

The rest of the week droned by in an exhausting manner. Between work at Sequence Inc., and work with my relationship with Kristen, I managed to find an opportunity to talk to the Dean at Brown to explain my situation. He was surprised to see how far my work ethic had taken me up the corporate chain and was sympathetic to the dilemma at hand. He allowed my admittance back to Brown on a provisional basis, meaning I was required to take a certain number of units in order stay eligible as a student at the ivy league level. Thanks to Lady Luck, my classwork was set to begin during the summer, since spring semester had already started and it was a minute too late to register for any classes.

When the night of the corporate party came around, my physical features looked more exhausted than before. A quick nap would've been helpful but I had promised Mr. Andrews I would arrive prior to greet the guests.

"Does my tie match?" I yearned for Kristen's fashion advice.

The side of her mouth turned slightly to the side as she examined my suit. After a moment she shrugged in approval. "You look handsome. That's all that matters right?"

I laughed uneasily.

Kristen didn't know whom I would be meeting at this party. Just the thought was enough to trigger sweat beads to break across the top of my forehead.

"Aren't you getting ready a little early?" Kristen teased when I didn't respond.

I straightened down my sleeves and shot her a grimace. "I have to arrive early to meet and greet. You'll catch a cab there right?"

"U-uh yeah of course," she stuttered.

"Is something the matter?"

She exhaled. "No, not at all."

I half-expected her try a little harder to communicate with me, but Kristen didn't say a word. Like me, maybe her feelings weren't as strong as she thought.

When the clock struck seven, I smoothed out my coat and told Kristen I would see her later at the party. Mr. Andrews was already there along with a couple other faces I recognized. Instinctively, my gaze flickered around for my peers—forgetting that this party was exclusive and I wouldn't be seeing anyone lower than a manager's position. I lounged around for a few minutes unsure what to do, Mr. Andrews was busy conversing with two other men—one, was short, balding, and, from the look of his face, slightly pompous. The other man stood about the same height as my boss but his expression was more controlled, or better yet, reserved. I trapped Mr. Andrews' gaze long enough for him to politely excuse himself. He strutted towards me and stopped a few feet short of personal contact. "Blake, the rest of the guests should be arriving soon." He kept the instructions brief. "Stand by the door and welcome them and don't forget to introduce yourself. Your name will be familiar to them."

I nodded compliantly and acquired a good footing at the door. One by one, and in groups of twos and threes, people filed in. I kept a smile on my face as I introduced myself to each and every one of them. The corporate heads recognized my name and yet, paid little attention to my accomplishments. By the end of the hour, everyone who was supposed to show up had, but with one exception, Kristen wasn't on my arm.

As the night progressed, so did my mood. I felt irritated that she had the nerve to blow off my big night, but a part of me knew I was being irrational—she probably caught an earlier flight or something.

"I thought you were bringing someone?" Mr. Andrews pulled me to the side.

I exhaled sharply. "I guess she couldn't make it." I tried to hide the chagrin.

He gave me a pat on the back. "Come, I'll like you to meet some people."

The rest of the night passed by successfully and I was sure an impression was made. I cracked jokes, listened to worse than boring stories with delight, and even managed to shake hands with some of the most important people there. When the night was finally over, the moon shined brightly overhead as I marched my way home. The minute I closed the door behind me, I half-expected Kristen to be around somewhere.

"Guess she really did get an earlier flight," I said to myself.

After a second of deliberation, I pulled out my phone and called her. Her phone went straight to voicemail, which I thought was odd until I realized she probably had to turn it off on the plane. I waited a few hours, busying myself with reading ahead for class before trying again. Just like the many times before, it was dead on the other line. I shrugged, thinking it was only a weekend, which meant she would be home in no time. I comforted myself with that thought.

I didn't realize how much I missed Kristen until I was lying in bed by myself. I sighed deeply, feeling the sting of loneliness as I draped the blanket tight around my shoulders. Random thoughts weaved through my mind and at one point I caught myself wondering how Finn and Pam were doing—that maybe I should give them a call...

No.

I discarded that idea and tried to sleep, throwing a pillow over my face.

The morning of Sunday I acted on my first impulse, but when I checked my phone, a wave of disappointment hit me. I gave out a little moan as I stared down at the empty screen, wondering why Kristen hadn't bothered to call me.

Did I do something wrong?

No, I shouldn't confuse myself.

Things were going great, I told myself. There was no possible reason for her not to call. Wasn't I supposed to get her from the airport or don't I deserve the decency of a message telling me she was staying another day or two?

Anger boiled inside of me and I allowed it, letting it leech off my energy and at the same time, effectively cleansing the disappointment right out my system. I scrambled to my feet and lumbered out the door. Halfway out of our apartment, I realized I didn't have a destination in mind. I shrugged, not caring where I went. I just had to be moving.

My feet became the decision makers as my mind was latched onto a different task. Two thoughts warred endlessly, the first one screamed to learn what I did wrong, and the other retorted with disgust as to why I was so pathetic and needy. I sighed deeply and finally looked up, surprised to see my steps had carried me into town. I walked more slowly, straining my eyes to see if anything appealed to me. But nothing did, so I continued to wander aimlessly. The anger walk proved to be taxing on my weakened body. The weather wasn't helping either. I shot a glare towards the sun, grimacing at the sweltering hot rays that beamed down on my exhausted body. A few hours crept by without my awareness and I figured it was time to go home. If I could still call it a home, that is.

I lay on the bed and threw an arm over my face. My eyelids drooped like window shades that desired to close off sunlight. After a long sigh, I let myself drift away to dreamland or nightmare town, I couldn't be sure.

The sound of the hard thumping on my door tossed me back to reality. I took a quick glance at the time and let out a groan. I threw my legs over the bed and slowly pulled myself upright before lumbering out the bedroom.

"Can I help you?" I pulled the door open a sliver.

"Are you the current resident living here?" the man said harshly.

I narrowed my eyes in suspicion. "Who's asking?"

He gave a small sigh and pressed his hand up against the door. I gripped the knob and trapped his gaze before I allowed his entry. "My name is Vincent Wilcox. And the purpose of my visit concerns Kristen Herter."

"I'm sorry but she's not in right now." I shook his hand and led him to the kitchen table.

Wilcox shook his head. "I work with the police department and I'm sorry to be the bearer of bad news but Ms. Herter was involved in a car accident."

At that moment, I could've sworn my heart stopped beating. Any negative feeling I felt before was completely enveloped by a new more powerful emotion: despair. I opened my mouth to react but all that came out was short gasps of air. It wasn't because I was incapable of registering the information, but rather, it made so much more sense that my instincts refused to believe it.

"H-how...when did this happen?" I croaked out.

"She was brought into the Miriam hospital on Saturday night."

My eyes blurred and the pit in my stomach erupted, putting further strain on my disorientation. It was my fault she was hurt, if I had left with her to the company party she wouldn't have been in this accident.

"What is the status of her condition?" I tried to collect myself in front of Wilcox.

He didn't answer immediately. Instead, his eyes shifted left and right uncomfortably. "She's in critical condition. The doctors don't think she'll make it." His tone was hard and sure.

I shook my head. "That's impossible. That can't be right."

"The car had no time to stop. Ms. Herter must've tripped and fallen into oncoming traffic, an unfortunate accident in everyone's eyes." Wilcox gave a small sigh.

I caressed the side of my forehead, trying to make this reality a nightmare. Any second now, Kristen would come through the door and climb into bed with me. I don't know how long I stayed in my diluted fantasy, but at one point, I heard a small "sorry" followed by a door closing. After another moment in limbo, my eyes fluttered open and glared down at my watch. Doc Primo had stated that I can only travel as far back as seventy-two hours, but I needed to go further to save Kristen. I gulped, knowing I had to try going back a full four days.

I exhaled in anticipation and closed my eyes before jamming my finger into the red button. After a second I jerked them open and looked left and right.

Nothing happened.

I was in the same exact spot and time I was in now: wallowing at my kitchen table. I pressed the red button again but the result was the same, I couldn't travel that far back.

I got up furiously and flipped the table over. What was the point of having this power if I couldn't save the one person closest to me? Was this really meant for only my own selfish desires? And then something happened that was long overdue, I snapped.

I screamed into the empty apartment—part from frustration and part from agony. The explosion of pent up emotion hurled me to the floor and I lay there, curled into a ball, crying. I thought and tried to believe it wasn't true but my body reacted differently. It knew Kristen was gone and that I would never see her again. My head coiled back and I recollected my last words to her, clearly mindful that it wasn't even an "I love you" it was a stupid "see you later".

After my tear ducts dried from crying, and after my throat grew hoarse from screaming, I stirred up what strength I had left to see Kristen one last time. I went across town to the Miriam Hospital. My steps felt sluggish and almost reluctant to approach the front desk. The receptionist must've saw my broken state because at that moment she grinned from cheek to cheek, a friendly smile to reassure me.

"Hello, I'm here to see Kristen Herter." My voice came out dry and weak.

Judging from her reaction she was familiar with Kristen's case. "What is your relationship to the patient?"

"I'm her boyfriend."

"I'm sorry, but right now it's only family."

Tears welled up and I pleaded desperately again.

Her face fell and she gave in. "She's in intensive care. Take the elevator to level 3 and make a right, that should take you to her."

I swallowed deeply and did as instructed.

Once on the third story I crossed the floor and made my way to the intensive care ward. My gaze bounced around restlessly, yearning to catch a glimpse of Kristen's name.

"Blake?" someone called to me.

I glanced in that direction and for a split-second I thought it was my girlfriend alive and well. But that fantasy was soon shattered as I drew closer. The woman in front of me was almost facially identical to Kristen but aged to a noticeable degree.

"Mrs. Herter," I said as a man came into view and draped his arm around her. "And Mr. Herter."

This was the first time I was meeting Kristen's parents. As fate would have it, I was meeting them under these circumstances. I assumed they recognized me through pictures their daughter had shown them. My eyes drowned in the weariness of their faces, the anguish in their expression, and their pained looks.

"How is she?" I blurted. I must've caught them by surprise because their eyes widening wasn't the reaction I was expecting.

Mrs. Herter tried to speak but it came out inaudible. Her husband gripped her shoulder tighter before clearing his throat. "Her heart is failing. There's nothing else that can be done." His tone was as shaky as my legs at that point. As I saw Kristen on her deathbed, my head spun with dismay and the rest of my body became disconnected with the world. I did the best I could to bear the stabbing pains that relentlessly attacked my heart.

"I'm so sorry..."

"It's not your fault, Blake, you didn't cause this accident," Mrs. Herter sobbed.

I felt pathetic—worse than pathetic—because it was my fault but I couldn't bring myself to tell them. After a moment, I felt a light shake on my shoulder. It was Kristen's father.

"You should go home. You shouldn't be forced to bear witness to her passing, leave that to us."

I nodded slowly and then turned away, my eyes shut tight to prevent any tears from escaping.

The days crept by, and by the end of the week, I was alerted of Kristen's passing and the date of her funeral. That same day, I remember vividly of crawling into her laundry and sobbing in it, finally unleashing all the guilt and anguish that had been boiling inside. After the first few breakdowns, my conscience felt slightly better, but even so, the nightmares were horrid. I felt pangs of anxiety every time I lay down. Even if I managed to get some shut-eye, I was wakened with nightmares of being in the hospital watching Kristen die.

The day of the funeral arrived; I took a cab to the place of the proceedings. My movements were slow as I entered the place, my gaze immediately falling on the casket at the front of the room. I don't know how long I stared for, but the next time I blinked, drops of water fell from my face and crashed down on the ground below. Many eyes bored into me, probably sympathetic to my despair.

No... I thought. I don't deserve your attention. I was the one who caused this...

I struggled to move my head forward, my movements tilting, and my vision blurred by the tears that were still pouring. A shiver ran down my spine and my body went into shock as I saw Kristen lying before me, eyes closed, body lifeless. I'd expected this, but yet, seeing it in real-time frightened me terribly. It didn't take much for the tears to build up again. I wiped my face with my sleeve before taking a step backwards. I found Mr. and Mrs. Herter in their seats, eyes puffier than the time of our first meeting.

I drew in a deep breath and staggered towards them. "I have no—" I couldn't continue, the shaking in my voice had grown uncontrollable.

A hand grazed the side of my cheek followed by a soothing maternal sound—the sound a mother would make to console a distressed child. I looked swiftly in that direction and was met with a pair of warm eyes.

"I'm glad you could make it," Mrs. Herter said. Her tone sounded hoarse—from crying I guessed. "You're a good person, I'm glad my little girl had the pleasure of meeting you in her lifetime."

15
Time never stops

I JOLTED UPRIGHT from the restlessness night. I glanced at the time, watching the secondhand cross the number twelve, indicating another minute had passed. I rubbed the sleepiness away and sat waiting for the paralysis in my legs to completely recede. My eyes shifted from my bed to the ground and then to the calendar.

It has been five years since Kristen left this planet but her presence still haunted my dreams, reshaping them to unsupervised nightmares. Life was moving at such a constant pace that grieving for a loved one too long was frowned upon. I took a few deep breaths to adjust my mind to reality before throwing my legs over the edge of the bed, and dragging my tender body to the shower. The aching intensified and I wondered how much more torment my body could handle. In other words, I'm already amazed by how far I'd gone. By recent month's time, my face grew considerably thin and aged well beyond my years. I even acquired a nickname at Sequence Inc., "geezer Dawson". It suited me just fine, I believed—my eyes were always droopy and my bones as brittle as a baby's.

The steaming water rained down on me for a good twenty minutes. It drenched my thinning hair and flowed down my scrawny body. I turned off the nozzle, dried myself and found my way to the kitchen, but not before stopping to center the photo frame of my diploma from Brown.

That's right. I was an Ivy League graduate with an executive position at one of the biggest companies in the world. All of this had been accomplished in five years time. Yes, five years. I couldn't remember the last time I really sat down and wondered if I was happy with my life, but who had time to do that anyways?

As I retrieved a bowl from the cupboard I fought my shaking hands. At first, it was amusing to think that a twenty-six year old could contract arthritis but now, it was a continuous struggle that I had to live day-to-day with. I chowed down the food as best I could without spilling before getting dressed and tethering Time Waver to my wrist. I tilted my head to the side as I examined my watch and how it still looked perfectly new, practically identical to the day I got it. This watch might be out of time's boundary.

I chuckled, the theory was entirely plausible—it did have power to travel on father time's linear rope after all. I entertained different thoughts, like how much time I had left, and whether I considered this power to be a burden or a gift. My gaze fell on the clock again, listening to the sound of the rhythmic ticking.

I struggled to get upright. I exhaled sharply, grabbed my coat and headed out into the morning mist. As my steps fell in line with the rest of the morning-bird flock, I figured I might as well walk all the way to Sequence Inc. A little exercise couldn't hurt after all. So I trekked along the sidewalk, passing things I never fully appreciated, like the sight of fresh hot dogs sizzled by the morning vendor, and the sound of flapping wings desperately escaping the noise of soon-to-be rush hour traffic.

By the time I wandered through the front doors and into my private office, I was exactly on time. I settled into work, making sure the data for international sales was precise and on point with the domestic sales. It didn't take long before my worker bees filed in, some twice as old as me and I was their boss. I snickered at this fact but the sudden amusement clogged my throat and resulted in a barrage of coughing.

My door opened followed by a soft-spoken voice. "Are you alright, Mr. Dawson?" It was my assistant. "Would you like some water?"

"No, I'm alright. Thank you, though." I cleared my throat.

"Oh, and you have mail from Mr. Andrews." She handed me a folder and then left.

I tore open the folder, examining the contents of it before resting on a personal message from Mr. Andrews himself. He wanted to extend his congratulations towards my excellent job performance. I chuckled at how impersonal his message sounded—while I'd taken over his job here, he was promoted to a senior executive position and was now somewhere in California basking in the sunny skies and clear-ocean views.

Suddenly, a sharp pain attacked my side. It lasted a fraction of a second and was soon followed by a numbing sensation. I grasped my side, and widened my eyes at how tender it felt.

I rubbed my forehead noticing clammy sweat breaking free but instantly vaporizing. But the attacks didn't stop. Consistent pains shot up and down my left arm as my heart drummed to irregular beatings. I tried to call out for help but my breath was short and shallow.

Was it a heart attack?

Yes, my brain told me.

I was going through a cardiac arrest and just like how I woke this morning, my body felt weak as paralysis took over my limbs. I drew in a deep breath and with every ounce of focus and strength I had left, I raised my arthritic hand and buzzed for my assistant. My mind did its best to wrap around reality but the allure of darkness was so enticing that my eyes fell backwards and my body flopped on the desk. Everything after that became a dark blur.

I twitched myself awake and found myself lying underneath bright fluorescent lights. Any normal person would deduce where they were in a matter of seconds, but for me it took an abnormal amount of time. If I wasn't confusing reality with some twisted dream, I was sure I was in a hospital room. My body still felt weak but I managed to pull myself slightly upright and rubbed my forehead.

"What the hell happened?" I snapped.

But no one was around to hear me. I was alone in here like I will be alone for the rest of my days. I exhaled heavily before lying back down, taking my time examining my condition. To the left was a vase of flowers with a card that read "Get well soon, love everyone in the office".

I laughed but stopped when my breath drew short and my chest emitted sharp pains. The card wasn't particularly humorous but it was disappointing that there wasn't a single signature. Now whom am I supposed to give the credit to?

I grinned, amused, and glanced upwards at my blood pressure and heart rate monitors. Both looking steady, or so I assumed. Without having anything else to do, I felt a sudden wave of exhaustion and decided to drown in it. I rested my eyes and drew the covers tight across my shoulders, letting sleep hit me like moving train.

"Blake?"

The voice sounded familiar, almost warm and invigorating.

"Blake?" It said again and this time I managed to flicker my eyes open, tracing the person's face.

I froze in shock when I made the mental connection with the owner of that dreamy voice.

Pam was staring at me with the same concerned expression I went through high school with. But the shock didn't end there. Standing behind her was someone I also knew very well. For the first time in seven years, Pam, Finn and I were in the same room again.

"Wh-what are you guys doing here?" I struggled to sit upright.

Pam flew to my side. A slight tingle ran up and down my spine as her warm fingers made contact with my skin.

"We're here to see how you are doing, silly." She spoke in a soothing voice.

My gaze flickered from Pam to Finn.

"How did you guys know I was here?" I said quietly.

"Some old dude told us," Finn shot me a small grin.

I kept my eyes on Finn for another second before resting them on Pam.

I exhaled sharply. "Some old guy?"

"Yeah, he called and told us you were in here," Pam fluffed my pillows as Finn got comfortable in one of the chairs. "We didn't believe him at first...but Finn called the hospital just to make sure, and it turns out the man wasn't lying."

"His name was Doc Primo or something weird like that," Finn commented.

I widened my eyes in shock before noticing my naked wrist. I had totally forgot about Time Waver and the rest of my possessions. Without a second's hesitation I buzzed in a nurse and asked where my things were.

"In your beside table drawer, sir." She seemed surprised by my sudden bewilderment.

I reached over with my hand but it was swiftly smacked away by Pam. "You need to lie still and rest. Let me get it for you."

I shot her a grimace but redirected it towards Finn as he bellowed with laughter.

"What is that you want, Blake?" Pam chirped, drawing my attention away.

"Uh, the watch, please."

She fumbled through the drawer for a moment before picking out Time Waver by its band. I extended my palm face-up and she dropped it.

"I'm surprised you still have that. Ever since senior year in high school, right?" Pam noted.

I nodded hesitantly.

"He loves that watch or something, I never saw him take it off while I was dorming with him either."

This time I laughed. Pam and Finn were next to me again, and for some odd reason, my mind couldn't accept the fact they were both here. They looked practically the same, except their choice of wardrobe had matured. Pam was laced in a pencil skirt and a blouse that emphasized her hips while Finn wore something that was part of a suit ensemble. Seeing them after such a long period of time sent a wave of guilt slamming against my insides.

"Guys, I just want to say—"

Finn cut me off. "Chill out, bro, it's all in the past. I knew you couldn't handle Brown!" he joked, shaking his head in pretend disappointment.

Pam rolled her eyes. "What Finn means is that we all just got really busy. We couldn't help it if we drifted a little." Pam smiled warmly.

I frowned, the fault rested on my shoulders. Pam and Finn caught the tension and quickly shifted topics.

"How does Sequence Inc. treat its employees for you to end up like this?" Finn scratched the back of his head.

"The job is pretty stressful and I never get enough rest, so exhaustion probably just caught up to me," I lied, gritting my teeth together.

Pam tilted her head in confusion and rested her hand on my forehead. The rest of my body cooled underneath her touch and warmed my cheeks instead. "I think you have a small fever but you should really give yourself a break from work once in a while!" she scolded.

I grimaced, which caused Finn to snicker again. "Better listen to Pam. She is a nurse now."

I looked up at her. "You're a nurse?"

"Yes. Shut up. I wanted to do something that would help people," She blushed a little. "But what's important is how you're feeling. I still can't believe someone your age had a heart attack." Pam shifted the focus back on me again.

I shrugged. "Unlucky I guess."

"Or impressive, is more like it!" Finn shot a wink in my direction.

"Impressive?" Pam shrieked. "Me punching you in the face would be impressive!"

Finn and I exchanged looks, his eyes narrowing in confusion because her insult made no sense whatsoever. It took her a moment to think about it before she scowled at us.

I wasn't quite sure how I felt at that point—it was an unsettling feeling that almost mimicked happiness. How uncanny. Time that used to crawl by had suddenly sprouted wings and taken flight. Before the grin on my face was completely wiped away, visiting hours were depressingly over.

"You two can come back tomorrow," the nurse poked her head in from the door.

Pam and Finn stumbled to their feet.

"What she said, we'll be back tomorrow," Finn said sleepily.

I nodded glumly and settled back down.

"Rest up, Blake," Pam leaned down for a quick hug.

"I will. Thanks for stopping by, guys."

Pam gave a small smile and Finn shrugged before they pulled the door open and turned the corner.

I closed my eyes and after a short while, felt myself drifting off. But as I lay there, eyes shut and mind wandering, I felt another presence in the room. It had to be my imagination I rationalized. No one was allowed in here anymore.

"Blake Dawson," someone said, their voice eerie but familiar.

The sound of my name sent a pang of terror that shook my eyes open. Standing at the foot of my bed was none other than Doc Primo, alive and in the flesh.

"Wh-what are you doing—"

"I'm here to see you, Blake."

I sat up and trapped his gaze. We didn't speak for the longest time, which was strange because I had a million questions to ask. "Is there a reason why you're here now?" I blurted.

"Yes."

I swallowed deeply. "Why did you send Pam and Finn to see me?"

Doc Primo paused and then recollected himself. "I thought it would be nice for you to see them one last time," he said calmly.

"What! One last time?"

"You're going to die tonight."

I couldn't register his words as the rest of my body froze in place. Meanwhile Doc Primo eyed me with a mixture of amusement and fascination. I expected to die much earlier but this soon? I wasn't ready.

"Hold the watch in your palm, Blake. I want to show you something."

"What?"

"I want to show you what your life would have been like if you never used Time Waver. Or better yet, hadn't used it for your own selfish gains."

A score of remorse slithered down my body and left a trail of regret in its wake. It was true what Doc Primo had said: I've exploited the ability to time travel for my own means, but in my defense, most people would too.

I did as he asked and flattened the watch in the palm of my hand. "What now?" I asked, my voice slightly shaking.

Doc Primo reached over and snatched Time Waver out of my hands. He tinkered around with it and then a split second later a little click sounded.

"Are you ready to see your life without this power?" His voice was low and hard.

I gulped, feeling unsure and curious at the same time. "Yes." I exhaled sharply.

The familiar whoosh attacked my ears and sent my body spiraling out of the hospital bed and into my high school years. I've heard the term out-of-body experience before but this was the epitome of it. I looked down at my outfit and realized I was still in my hospital gown. The arthritis in my hands had disappeared and my legs felt fresh and strong. I scanned the area, reminiscing my time here before Doc Primo tapped me on the shoulder.

"Follow me," he instructed as a student glided through his body like he was a ghost.

I trailed behind Doc Primo. Ahead, Pam, Finn, and myself crowded a table with books labeled *SAT prep*. I couldn't help but let out a laugh at how young I looked. But what caught my eye was my naked wrist. There was no watch wrapped around it, it was plain and in perfect skin tone with the rest of my body. I took a step towards the table and then another step, but someone gripped my shoulder and everything blurred away.

"Where are we now?" I asked, once my feet were safely planted on the ground.

"Look around, you'll know," Doc Primo said smoothly.

I wheeled around. I was in my old room. Lying in my bed was a young me.

"BLAKE!" a voice called my name.

Shock stung and jolted my body when I realized it was my mother. I staggered backwards as my other self rose up from the bed. "What is it?" he said.

"YOUR ADMISSION LETTERS ARE HERE!"

As if his life depended on it, my younger self leaped off the bed and rushed to the kitchen. I gasped and shot a look at Doc Primo. He gazed back sympathetically before leaving the room.

I took another moment to recollect myself before following suit.

"Open them right here!" My mom clasped her hands together.

"I don't know if I should... I kind of want some privacy, Mom," my younger self said, running his fingers through his hair.

I stared at them.

"What schools did I apply to?" I said without looking at Doc Primo.

"The same ones," he replied.

"What about Pam and—"

My mom cut my younger self off. "No, do it right here."

I strode by and glanced over my own shoulder as I peeled the letters open one by one. The top schools gave a rejection, but the school that really caught my eye, UCLA, sent a congratulations.

I sighed in relief and twirled to face Doc Primo. "What school would I be going to if Brown rejected me?" I mused, a small smile latching on my lips.

He raised an eyebrow. "Patience, Blake, time is all you have now."

I watched as my mom flushed over my past self's accomplishments. A moment later, he paced back into his room and I matched his footsteps. I stood by the wall, hearing a phone dial and then a second later Pam's voice sprang up on the other line. I listened to the conversation intensely, hearing the joy in "my" voice and Pam's when plans to attend UCLA together were finalized. The smile smacked on my former self's face was contagious, and blood shot up to my cheeks. I turned away from the scene but Doc Primo called me back.

"Enough of that, let's take a journey to your college years." He placed his hand on my shoulder and in a second, reality whisked by me again.

I flickered my eyes around, aware of the unfamiliar surroundings. I stared nervously at the dark sky, hesitating to ask where I was. "I don't recognize this place," I noted shortly.

"It's obvious you don't." Doc Primo paused to take a breath before continuing, "This is the campus of the college you were meant to go to. You've never visited Pam in your own timeline so of course you would have no idea where you are. But come on now, let's go find you."

I didn't bother to question Doc Primo's sense of direction; his swift steps were enough to tell me that he knew where he was going. We crossed the lawn to the dormitories, and found my room. Once inside I wasn't surprised by what I saw. Pam and UCLA Blake studying together, her on the bed and me at the desk. But what happened next virtually dislocated my jaw and forced it to drop.

The UCLA me dropped the textbook, stretched his arms and yawned before climbing into bed with Pam. She merely made room but gave no indication she was bothered. He wrapped his arm around her waist which made her whisper fiercely, "Now isn't the time to cuddle, I have a big exam tomorrow."

But he only gripped her tighter and her reaction the second time was unexpected. She broke out in giggles before falling into the embrace. It sounded stupid and almost in all cases impossible, but at that moment, I was jealous of myself. Unable to tear my eyes away, my focus lingered on these two, playfully wrestling each other before Pam straightened out her shirt and continued skimming through her notes.

I cocked my head to Doc Primo for answers. I didn't have to voice them because he already knew what I wanted to ask. "Yes, if you went to UCLA you would've been with Pam. She would've never had the time to meet Bruce." Doc Primo shot one look at my miserable face.

My arms went rigid at my side. Were my decisions in my own life truly worth it? All the money, power and prestige…was it really worth it if I had no one to share it with?

I trailed that thought and it led me to my past demons. In this life, I was with Pam, which meant I was never with Kristen. She wouldn't have died prematurely.

I actually look pretty happy, I thought glumly. Which makes sense; Pam was the source of that happiness.

Sensing my reluctance to stay and watch, Doc Primo sent us through time again. This moment we were back at my old home. I tilted my head into the kitchen and found my mom cooking dinner. It smelled delicious. Outside, snow was piling up quickly. It created a soft blanket on the black asphalt, altering manmade ugly into natural beauty. A door slammed and a second later, young Blake strutted in, hand curled around Pam's.

I swallowed deeply.

But that wasn't the only surprise. My dad came in and did something that almost brought tears to my dying eyes. He kissed my mother.

"What the hell?" I gasped. My legs gave out and eyes grew wet and disoriented.

Doc Primo stood by my side. "Since you never went to Brown, your dad never had the opportunity to meet...what was her name now?" He thought for a moment as he examined some photos hanging on the wall. "Ah, Ms. Terry. I believe that was her name. Well yes, he never met her so he and your mom never went through a divorce." He ended on that note, his tone light, as if those words wouldn't hurt me.

My head wrapped around his words. It was my fault that my parents got a divorce, it was my fault that they weren't together now like they are in this world. The conclusion stung, I had to admit, it seemed like every decision I made with Time Waver hurt everyone else, including me.

"So, what is today supposed to be?" I murmured, turning my head away from the family dinner. But even if I did look away, I couldn't shut my ears, the booming laughter and the chirpy talk were verbal happiness, to say the very least.

Doc Primo chuckled darkly behind me. "Just a regular night in your winter break. Nothing of a special occasion or anything of that sort."

I gave out a sigh and turned back to the dinner table. Prevalent thoughts swirled around my head but they all came to the same conclusion: I was happy in this timeline.

"Let's move on," Doc Primo said in exasperation. "We have more ground to cover."

I took a step forward and Doc Primo rested his hand on my shoulder before we leapt out of sight.

The next time I flickered my eyes open, it was to the sight of rows upon rows of white chairs. I furrowed my eyebrows and gazed curiously at my surroundings, balloons, tapering, and...an altar.

I jerked towards Doc Primo. "Is someone getting married?"

"You. Today is your wedding day." Doc Primo pointed with his index finger at the door where guests flocked in to find their seats as laughter and excitement chilled the sky above. It was a clear day, a warm day—a day perfect for an outside event such as this. I felt my body sway where it stood and my legs felt like jelly, wobbling to collapse. The doc and I fluttered to the side as the rest of the guests found their seats. I scanned the rows for familiar faces where I spotted a few. My parents looked well in later years, father graying but still masculine, and mother still had a sparkle in her smile. Pam's parents sat on the opposite side but were equally stunning. If possible, everyone looked better than I did now. A couple of chairs down, I caught a glimpse of people I've known since high school. My jaw dropped, stunned to see Cory Wraith and Amber Stone among them. But that wasn't the only surprise: Mr. Andrews was sitting in the adjacent row.

I pulled on Doc Primo's arm. "How did I meet Mr. Andrews if I never went to Brown?" I said, stunned.

He cleared his throat before speaking. "Not every-thing changed in your timeline. Mr. Andrews's destiny still remained the same and it brought him here to California."

"Wait, we're in California right now?"

"Yes, you and Pam live here now and you have a job at Sequence Inc. as a junior executive."

My gaze shifted left and right, partly out of confusion and partly because I couldn't believe it. It seemed like my life would've fallen into place by itself without me forcing it to.

"Well..." I started, pulling my arms flat by my sides. "Time Waver was really a curse after all, or at the very least, I made it that way," I finished before my jaw locked tight.

Doc Primo nodded, understanding. But his eyes told me differently. It seemed almost sympathetic, looking at me with compassion. But the glance was cut short as the wedding bells chimed, signaling the start of the ceremony. At the opposite end of the altar, I spotted Finn and a couple other guys I didn't recognize skulking around until my other self came into view. Finn and I embraced, and it was clear my best friend was my best man.

"You look good, huh?" Doc Primo whispered in my ear. "Your hair looks just fantastic."

I nodded and ran my hands through my receding hair-line, scowling in the process. It was true though, this alter-nate reality me was every bit I envisioned myself to be: confident, healthy, with a good job, good friends, and most of all, the girl of his dreams.

As the groom and his entourage strolled down the walkway, all chatter and noise went dead. It wasn't until they reached the altar that fierce whispering erupted. Moments later, the bell chimed again and this time, everybody stood from their seats. A goddess glided in, body covered in a white dress that accented her shapely frame, and face hidden by a thin veil. But still, the most beautiful thing about Pam was her smile. It radiated like a sun that couldn't be hidden by clouds. The action of blinking ceased as I watched attentively as Pam and I stood shoulder-to-shoulder, ready to enter a forever commitment.

"Do you Blake, take this girl to be your wedded wife, in sickness and in health, and till death do you part?" The minister looked left to right.

I curled my hands around Pam's. "Not even death will we part."

A small smile formed on her lips as the minister repeated his words for the bride-to-be.

"Not even death will we part," Pam repeated, still smiling.

A small break of silence followed but it ended just as quickly.

"Then I now pronounce you husband and wife!" the minster cried.

The place erupted in cheering, clapping, and surprisingly, a couple of whimpers. Even I couldn't resist the tears forming in my eyes as Pam and I locked in an embrace tighter than the rings on our fingers.

"I think I've seen enough," I managed to croak out as the newlyweds rejoiced with the guests.

"Certainly," was all Doc Primo said.

I wiped my eyes and a few seconds later, I was right where I belonged, dying on the hospital bed. The physical aching and pain returned, pricking my body with small doses of torment. I couldn't endure the emotional trauma I had just experienced. My life would've been perfect. That thought hit me and I began half-bawling and half-laughing, a mixture of sorrow and amusement in the greatest sense.

"Is something particularly funny, Blake?" Doc Primo asked.

I couldn't stop laughing, only pausing at times because my lungs were throbbing, but other than that, I merely waved at Doc Primo and pointed at myself.

"You find your situation comedic," he assumed. "Well, I guess you understand what that trip was about then."

After a moment, I regained enough control to wipe the tears from my eyes. In the few seconds of silence, my heartbeat slowly receded before attaining a weak rhythm.

"It was a test and I failed," I muttered.

Doc Primo nodded and then said, "I told you from the beginning to use it carefully, but you succumbed to human nature."

"If that's human nature then you knew I would fail?"

"No, that simply means you had a greater probability of failing, but there's no guarantee in life. I have hope and still believe that human nature can change."

I took a moment to digest the information, but as my mind raced my heart slowed.

When I didn't respond, Doc Primo spoke again, "Don't feel too bad, no one has passed this test yet."

I looked up at him. "There were others before me?"

"Yes, twenty-four previous owners of this watch. All of them had helped me out of some predicament so in return, I gave them this gift."

"Curse is more like it." I snorted.

Doc Primo coiled his hand around the watch, brushing the glass screen with his thumb. "Ah, but you see, Blake, it's all a matter of perception. In the beginning you found this power to be a gift, but nearing your end, you see it as a curse." Doc Primo paused to stroke the watch again. "But that's true of life itself now, isn't it? Some see it as a gift and others see it as torment."

I laughed, as my body had grown numb. I didn't have too much time left, I presumed. "What is the point you're trying to make? How we perceive things leads to understanding it?"

"Precisely."

"I don't understand."

"You first saw Time Waver as a gift and you therefore abused it, but if you saw it as a curse from the beginning, you would have stayed away, wouldn't you?"

"True."

The numbing intensified to dangerous levels. Considering that I couldn't move any part of my body told me the end was coming. "Was that the main point you wanted to address?" My voice was hoarse.

"Somewhat. The second point was to teach you that everything happens for a reason. Blake, you saw first-hand what your life would've been like if you lived it out without any interference. But you mutilated time for your own self-benefit and that backfired. Sure, it looked like life was going well but the cost you had to pay. Was it worth it now?"

I didn't have to think. "No, it wasn't worth it."

"Exactly, because everything happens for a reason."

Wave after wave of exhaustion slammed into me, forcing my body to go rigid. Out of the corner of my eye, Doc Primo had turned and swiftly walked towards the door, dropping Time Waver into his coat pocket.

"What are you going to do now?" I struggled to keep my eyes open for a few more seconds.

"Continue my search to find someone who can prove me wrong about human nature. Goodbye, Blake Dawson."

"I wish you luck."

Doc slipped out and disappeared.

The fatigue became unbearable and I no longer wished to fight it. My body had already given out—the only thing keeping me chained to this life was the regret that swallowed me. I didn't want to sound cliché but Doc Primo was right in saying everything happens for a reason. Me in this position was the result of that. I gave a half-smile as my gaze lingered out the window for one more look before closing forever, allowing every piece of my existence: body, mind, and spirit to become a tiny speck in time and all of its power.

Author Biography

 Daniel Doan lives in Garden Grove, California. He attended the University of California, Irvine and earned his Bachelor's Degree in Criminology, Law and Society. *Time Waver* is his first published novel. His author website is listed below. Check it regularly for future updates!
www.danielqdoan.com

Made in the USA
Charleston, SC
14 March 2015